THE TEXAS TATTLER

All the news that's barely fit to print!

Fortune Empires To Merge

International Business Deal Unites Family

Financial newsflash—What do you get when you combine Texas's and Australia's most successful ranching operations? A whole lotta honor, a whole lotta ego and a whole lot *more* money. Wall Street was reeling this week when word leaked that the mammoth Double Crown and Crown Peak ranches will merge, creating the single largest ranching outfit in history. *Investors, Inc.* says "Fortune" is now *the* name in ranching.

The deal will skyrocket the Fortune power and wealth to astounding proportions, though it is still too early for solid predictions about the impact on the family's net worth. But one thing's for sure...if these folks keep merging, marrying and mothering at this rate, they're going to give a whole new meaning to Fortune 500!

And on to "love news"...*The Tattler's* fashion guru couldn't help but notice the sudden, drastic change in Teddy Fortune's only daughter, Matilda. She has traded in her dusty overalls for utterly elegant duds. Could all this focus on her femininity have something to do with exec-to-swoon-for Dawson Prescott? A source *amazingly* close to the famed family says that Dawson has tried to resist the tomboy-turned-tantalizer, but recent late-night "developments" (involving a boudoir, a shotgun and an ultimatum) might mean one more Fortune will soon bite the marriage dust!

 Meet the Fortunes of Texas

Matilda Fortune: From the moment Matilda met Dawson Prescott, he made her heart skip a beat. So the former tomboy transformed herself into a stunning, self-assured woman and hoped the new-and-improved Matilda could win his heart.

Dawson Prescott: When he was found in a compromising position with Matilda, he dutifully married her. Would his new bride turn out to be the perfect wife he hadn't known he was looking for?

Griffin Fortune: The secret agent didn't think of himself as the marrying kind. But when he was asked to protect an innocent beauty, he began to second-guess his bachelor status....

SHOTGUN
Vows

TERESA SOUTHWICK

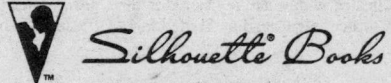

Published by Silhouette Books

America's Publisher of Contemporary Romance

Special thanks and acknowledgment are given
to Teresa Southwick for her contribution
to THE FORTUNES OF TEXAS series.

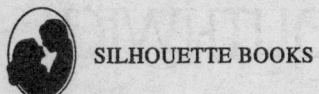 **SILHOUETTE BOOKS**

ISBN 0-373-21747-1

SHOTGUN VOWS

About the Author

TERESA SOUTHWICK

At the tender age of ten, Teresa Southwick learned to deal with rejection when her four brothers found and "critiqued" one of her medieval stories. Then she could tattle to Mom, who unfortunately didn't send the blackguards to the gallows, or at the very least the dungeon, as Teresa had hoped. But it would be almost thirty years before she would again put pen to paper—or more accurately, fingers to keyboard.

A California girl born and raised, she spent many blissful hours sitting on the beach reading romance novels. Her fondness for happy endings began with Nancy Drew, and if she'd written those stories, Nancy and Ned would be living happily ever after. The good news is that her fascination with a wonderful love story was alive, well and flourishing in spite of her brothers.

She sold her first book in 1993, and in 1995, she achieved her longtime goal of writing for Silhouette Romance. The best part of writing, she believes, is that there are always more challenges around the corner. When she was asked to participate in THE FORTUNES OF TEXAS series, she jumped at the chance to write *Shotgun Vows*. The experience of working with such a talented and generous group of writers was both daunting and rewarding. The best part was sharing the news with her brothers—blackguards matured into heroes—who never miss a chance these days to brag about their "famous" sister.

Teresa and her husband have two grown sons.

To THE FORTUNES OF TEXAS authors.
It's been a pleasure and a privilege working with
a talented, generous group of writers.
I'm grateful to be included in your ranks.

One

It was rumored that Griffin Fortune knew three hundred ways to kill with his bare hands. How could you say no to someone like that?

"You're absolutely sure you want me to watch out for your sister?" Dawson Prescott asked again.

He studied Griffin, sitting across the desk from him. Dawson wasn't afraid of him; he was a friend. In spite of Griff's dangerous reputation, Dawson liked him and his brothers. It was their sister, Matilda, who rubbed him the wrong way.

Griff brushed a hand over his dark brown hair. The short, military cut didn't move. "You heard me right," he said. His Australian drawl did nothing to soften the words. If anything, his "down under" accent added intimidation. "I want you to watch over Mattie while I'm gone. We had this discussion already."

"Yeah, I remember," Dawson said. "I just didn't think you were serious." *Hoped* he wasn't serious would be more accurate. But Dawson suspected Griff never said anything he didn't mean.

"Dead serious," he answered, confirming the suspicion. "If I could put off this job, I would." He met Dawson's gaze squarely and a predatory glint crept into his brown eyes. "But I have to go."

Dawson knew he would say no more about it than that.

Here in the plush carpeted, wood-accented office at Fortune TX, Ltd. where he worked as a financial analyst, it was hard for Dawson to imagine what the other man did when he disappeared. But Dawson had quickly come to like and respect him. Whatever it was that took the man out of town, Dawson instinctively knew Griffin Fortune was one of the good guys.

Dawson pushed his cushy leather chair away from the desk, leaned back, and linked his hands over his abdomen. "But again I have to ask—why me? My baby-sitting skills leave something to be desired."

"If she were a baby, we wouldn't be having this conversation," Griff said, his Aussie drawl thickening with irony.

As much as he wanted to, Dawson couldn't argue with the fact that Matilda Fortune was no baby. Every time he heard her name, he instantly thought of her long, shapely legs encased in denim—followed quickly by a flash of those legs wrapped around his waist. He'd only ever seen her in work clothes with her shirt pulled out and hanging loose. If the rest of her was as good as those legs, and he ever got a look at the package, they would all be in trouble.

The weird thing was that in the looks department she was nothing to write home about. Ordinary braided blond hair, average gray eyes, and pale skin all added up to a woman as plain as her name: Matilda. Who thought that up? Dawson only knew that she pushed some of his buttons—all of them wrong. But it was unlikely that anything personal would ever happen with her. Ever since they had laid eyes on each other, sparks had flown between them—and not the good kind.

"Correct me if I'm wrong," he said, "but isn't she twenty-one? Why does she need looking after?"

"She's been sheltered. She trusts everyone and has never met a stranger. My four brothers and I have always watched out for her. But she's changed since she got to Texas. What do you people put in the water?"

Dawson blinked. "Excuse me?"

"There's something going around and it's called Matrimony. Seems to be catching. Soon my brother Brody and Jillian will be tying the knot. But it all started with my brother Reed when he married your sister."

Dawson and his half sister Mallory hadn't grown up together. Different mothers. But his gut told him his sister's match with Griff's brother was a good one. "I've never seen her happier."

"Reed, too." One corner of Griff's mouth lifted as he sat up straighter in the chair. "On top of that, Mattie's been acting strange ever since she found out that Jillian is going to have a baby. I overheard her tell Jillian that she wants one of her own soon. I wouldn't put it past her to run off with one of the ranch hands at the Double Crown."

Dawson couldn't remember ever hearing Griff string together that many sentences. Obviously the guy was really concerned. With a sister of his own, Dawson could understand the protective instinct. But he was a financial analyst for crying out loud. Granted, he worked for the family company, Fortune TX, Ltd. But surely they wouldn't expect him to nursemaid Matilda Fortune, the troublemaker cousin from Australia.

The assignment was definitely above and beyond the call of duty. He worked on spreadsheets... Bad choice of words. Instantly he thought of Matilda's long legs and tangled bed sheets. Damn, this was a bad idea. He'd agreed reluctantly, and only because he'd never actually expected Griff to take him up on it. Now he wished he'd never said yes.

The question was how he could gracefully get out of this. *Here goes,* he thought ruefully.

"She doesn't like me much, Griff. Surely you've noticed. If looks could kill, I'd be a chalk outline on the floor. Wouldn't it be better if you found someone else for guard duty?"

"There are three things that make you an ideal candidate for this assignment." Dawson didn't miss the harnessed strength in the other man's wrist and forearm as he held up three fingers. "One—Reed is on his honeymoon, and Brody is too preoccupied with his own upcoming wedding and becoming a father in a couple of months to do the job justice. Two—you're practically a Fortune, being my cousin Zane's friend and all. Three—you're right. She hates your guts." He grinned. "That makes you perfect for the job, mate."

"I've got number four."

"What's that?" he asked.

"She's just a kid."

He was eleven years her senior, a fact he'd pointed out at his first meeting with the Australian she-devil. Not that he was old. She'd figured that out all by herself. They'd accompanied Reed and Mallory to the rodeo. All Dawson had said was that he hadn't expected Reed's sister to be so young. That had instantly gotten Matilda's back up, and she'd fired off her own verbal shot.

Even if Dawson were attracted to her—at least the "her" that was separate from those dynamite legs—the disparity in their ages was something he would never get past. After his parents had split up, his father had married a much younger woman—a fact that had angered and embittered his mother. She'd had her nose rubbed in the fact that she was no longer young and had no weapons to fight for her man. Dawson had vowed that he would never use a woman and toss her aside like yesterday's meat loaf. Furthermore, he would never make the same mistakes his father had.

He wasn't like his father. He would never be like him.

Griff nodded. "By process of elimination as well as default, you're the ideal candidate."

Dawson knew he had no choice, and the thought rankled. He wasn't a man who liked being backed into a corner. "How long are you going to be gone?"

Griff shrugged. "There's no way to know for sure. I'll do my best to get back before Brody and Jillian's wedding."

That was just over three weeks away, the weekend before Thanksgiving. Dawson figured he could handle Matilda Fortune that long.

He nodded slowly. "I'll make sure she doesn't run off with a cowboy."

"Good. One favor, Dawson."

"I'm already doing you a favor."

"Then do yourself one. Don't let Mattie know what you're up to."

"She wouldn't like it?"

Griff laughed, but there was no humor in the sound. "That's an understatement. She doesn't like being treated like a kid. She's a grown woman, she says."

"Yeah, that message got through loud and clear," Dawson commented.

"Then if you know what's good for you, don't let on that I asked you to keep an eye on her."

"I'll do my best," he promised.

Satisfied, Griff held out his hand. "I owe you, mate."

And then some, Dawson thought, hoping he wouldn't live to regret this. It was the first of November and the promise he'd made just about guaranteed that he could kiss off having only good days for three-quarters of the month.

Matilda Fortune listened to the *clunk* of her boots on the foyer tile as she made her way to the Double Crown Ranch's great room. She stopped when her heels sank into the thick carpet. The large open hearth held a cheery fire. On the other wall, French doors opened to one of the house's two courtyards. Large leather couches and comfortable chairs in groupings that invited intimate conversation were arranged in several places in the large room.

Since her arrival from Australia several months ago, she found it was her uncle Ryan and aunt Lily's custom to spend the evening in the great room. Tonight was no exception. They were sitting side by side on one of the leather sofas, having after-dinner drinks with their other houseguest, Willa Simms. She was Ryan's goddaughter. Willa's father and Ryan had been best friends in Vietnam, a bond that remained strong until her dad died of cancer. She was still very close to Uncle Ryan—like one of his children.

Through an archway to her right she could see the dining room and the living room beyond. A huge painted armoire, and Western-style pieces including antler lamps and Native American prints, gave the room warmth and personality. She liked the house in spite of its intimidating size and the fact that she always felt as if she brought the outdoors inside as soon as she walked in.

Mattie moved farther into the room until she faced her aunt and uncle. "I didn't see Griff's car outside. Does anyone know where my brother is?"

She knew the answer even as the words came out of her mouth. If Griff's car were here, she would have known his whereabouts. He was joined at the hip with her. Her shadow. Her keeper. If his car was gone, he must be on one of his mysterious trips.

"He left on business, dear," her aunt said, confirming Mattie's guess. "He wasn't sure when he would be back, but asked me to tell you not to worry."

"From his mouth to God's ear." Mattie whispered her usual fervent prayer.

Telling her not to worry was like asking the wind not to blow. Griff would never confide details to anyone in the family about what he did when he was away. He said the less they knew, the better. How could they not worry when someone they loved said *that?*

But she smiled at her aunt and uncle, not wanting to upset them or let anyone know her feelings. There was nothing they could do or say to ease her mind.

Mattie studied her aunt and uncle, thighs brushing while holding hands. As always, she was struck by what a handsome couple they were. She knew they were both in their early fifties, but neither looked it. Lily's eyes were the color of a moonless night, and her shiny black bob, along with the beautiful bone structure in her face, revealed her Spanish and Indian heritage. She was still a lovely woman and must have been a stunner as a young girl.

Uncle Ryan was definitely his wife's equal. With his dark eyes and hair showing a bit of gray at the temples, and a still-muscular physique, he must have made female hearts flutter in his younger days. And at least one female heart still fluttered, Mattie thought as she saw the glow in his wife's eyes as she looked up at him. The two were obviously in love, obviously soul mates.

Like her own parents.

Mattie sighed. Would she ever find someone who would love her like that? A man she could respect and care about and raise a family with? A soul mate of her own?

It was her most cherished dream. Unfortunately, her brothers frightened away anyone who showed even the slightest interest in her. That made it darn near impossible to make her fairy tale come true. If Prince Charming didn't have the guts to face down the Fortune brothers, then she didn't particularly want to set up housekeeping in his castle. No wimp for her!

When her aunt and uncle had visited Australia and invited her to their ranch in Texas, she'd thought it was the opportunity she'd been waiting for. She'd taken them up on the offer and fallen in love with the state, the air, the wide-open spaces. The *men* that all the wide-open spaces would hold.

Since horses were her life, where better to find the man of her dreams than a Texas ranch? So many cowboys, so little time. The bad news was that Griff never left her side. The steely-eyed looks he gave any man who even glanced in her direction were enough to make monks out of them.

But Griff was gone. What was that American saying? *Make hay while the sun shines.* How appropriate on a ranch! And she finally understood the meaning. She would worry terribly about Griff, but with him away, it was definitely hay-making time.

Tonight the Double Crown cowboys held their weekly poker game. She'd almost forgotten, having dismissed the earlier casual reminder because she knew there was no way Griff would let her go. Or worse, he would accompany her—and then no one would have any fun. This was her first chance to join in. Maybe she could finally get one of them to notice her.

"I'm sorry we couldn't hold dinner for you, dear," her aunt said.

"No worries," Mattie answered.

"I just love your accent," Willa chimed in. "It's so cute."

"Thanks." Mattie smiled at her, then looked back at her aunt and uncle. "I'm sorry to be so late. I just couldn't tear myself away."

"Your brothers say you have a way with animals, Mattie," Willa said. "They say when they have a problem horse, you're the one they go to. That's such a gift. I'm a little afraid of an animal big enough to stomp me into roadkill without a second thought."

"You traveled all over the world with your father, Willa," Uncle Ryan said. "There was never time or opportunity to learn about horses."

"I'd be happy to work with you and show you some tricks," Mattie said. "Then you would be more comfortable around them. There's no reason to be afraid of horses. I can find just the right animal—one with a nature as sweet as yours.''

Willa smiled. ''How I envy your ability to do that.''

Not as much as I envy you. Mattie barely held in a sigh. Willa was so petite and pretty. Even her wire-rimmed glasses couldn't disguise her beautiful blue-gray eyes. Tonight her shoulder-length auburn hair was secured on top of her head with a clip. Mattie made a mental note to ask how she did that. All thumbs herself, she never fussed with her hair. A braid was easy, fast, and worked just fine. That clip contraption wouldn't hold up when she was riding. But if she had a date, it could work just fine, she thought.

Lily sipped her brandy. ''Rosita put the leftovers in the fridge for you, Mattie.''

''Thank you.''

Then she was free. No big brother watching. Whatever was she going to do with all this independence? The pressure was on. She didn't know how long Griff would be gone. The possibilities were endless. But tonight there was that poker game. Exhilaration surged through her, lifting her spirits.

The coast was clear!

Rosita Perez, the Fortunes' sixtyish housekeeper, entered the room. Her black hair was pulled back, highlighting the one white streak that started at her forehead and disappeared into the bun at her nape. Mattie liked the motherly woman who dished out hugs almost as plentifully as food. The downside was that she was followed by a man in business clothes.

Mattie felt two parts excitement and one part irritation when she recognized Mr. Stuffed Shirt in the expensive suit. Dawson Prescott.

He hardly looked at her as he walked briskly past

her to Uncle Ryan and shook hands. He nodded to her aunt and Willa, then gave Mattie the briefest of glances. Boy, that chapped her hide. Just like their first meeting when he had said she looked eighteen. Ever since, he'd ignored her, as if she didn't exist. Every time she'd seen him around the Double Crown with her cousin Zane and her brothers, he hadn't even glanced her way. *Cheeky devil,* she thought. She tried not to let it bother her, but it damn well did.

"I brought the portfolios for you to look at, Ryan," he said to her uncle.

"Didn't I tell you that I trust your judgment? I've put together a dynamite staff, the best there is, one that I trust implicitly to handle money matters. Mostly family, I might add." He looked at Dawson. "Or practically family."

His wife smiled lovingly at him. "Didn't anyone ever tell you that pride, even in staff that is practically family, goes before a fall, my darling?" she teased.

He put his arm around her. "Yes. And when mine comes, it'll be a humdinger. I can only hope there's a bungee cord attached when it happens. But I trust Dawson. It wasn't necessary to bring this out here tonight."

Lily looked at the newcomer. "But since you did, the least we can do is feed you. Have you had dinner yet, Dawson?"

Tell her yes, Mattie said to herself. *Yes, yes, yes.*

"No, I haven't," Dawson answered. "But it's not necessary—"

"There are plenty of leftovers," Lily continued. "Can we warm something up for you?"

Say no, Mattie thought. *No, no, no.*

"That would be great," he said. "But I don't want to put you to any trouble."

Perverse man, Mattie thought. Completely ignored her mental telepathy. She would have to work on that.

"It's no trouble, dear," Lily said. "As a matter of fact, Matilda just walked in, and she hasn't had dinner yet, either. So now she won't have to eat alone." The older woman smiled brightly.

The evening had just gone downhill in a big way, Mattie decided. And it had started out so promising.... Now she was cornered. She wouldn't insult her family by not extending hospitality to another guest in their home. She would set a record for fast food-consumption, then say her farewells and head for the bunkhouse.

She forced herself to smile at Dawson. "I'm going to go clean up. Then I'll meet you in the kitchen."

"Don't rush, dear," Lily said. "We'll entertain Dawson while you freshen up."

During her shower and then a quick combing and braiding of her hair afterwards, all Mattie could think was, *Why me?* Why did she draw the short straw and get stuck with the dude? Although if she had to be stuck with someone she didn't like, at least he wasn't hard on the eyes. She hadn't been that close to him since their first verbal sparring. Then she'd been too annoyed to notice. But tonight, being in the same room with him, she couldn't miss the intensity that made his hazel eyes seem more green, or the way the light picked up the sunstreaks in his brown hair, or how wide his shoulders looked in that white dress shirt, wrinkled after a day's work.

"Work?" she said to herself, slipping on a clean pair of jeans. "Number cruncher," she said disdainfully as she put on a long-sleeved white cotton shirt. She couldn't think of a more boring or lonely way to make a living. In fact, she might even feel sorry for him—if he was anyone but Dawson Prescott.

She glanced one last time in the mirror, and sighed as she noticed the blond wisps of hair that curled around her face. No matter how hard she tried, her hair had a mind of its own. So she'd quit trying to make it do anything other than braid. Was it her imagination, or did her eyes look a deeper gray than usual? Must be the anticipation of that poker game, she thought.

Mattie made her way to the kitchen. The floor of the large room was tiled with Mexican pavers. A distressed-wood table with eight ladder-back chairs stood in a cozy nook at one end of the room. At the other end was a center island work area, a counter cooktop set into the cream-colored tiles, and a built-in oven. Not to mention the largest side-by-side refrigerator she had ever seen.

That was where she now saw Dawson, half bent at the waist as he scoped out the contents. She noticed that his gray slacks pulled tight across his legs, revealing muscular thighs. She wondered how he managed to produce all those muscles while poring over numbers all day.

"See anything good?" she asked.

"Lily and Ryan said to make myself at home," he answered, as he continued to study the interior.

Then he looked at her, and she thought his gaze lowered to just about her knees. No doubt he was trying to think of something to say to cut her off just about there. She resolved not to rise to any bait he might set out. She would be the lady her mother always scolded her into trying to be.

She pointed to the open door. "I think pot roast and mashed potatoes were on tonight's menu. If you'll allow me?"

He backed away with an outstretched palm. "Be my guest."

"Actually, I believe you're *my* guest."

"Look, Matilda—"

She held her hand up, palm out. "Stop right there, buster." She tried to add a teasing note to her voice. "My aunt expects us to keep each other company for this meal. That implies making conversation. To do that you need to get my attention. Especially if I have my back turned. I'll answer to 'Hey, you,' or 'Yo, babe.' You can even grunt if you'd like. But I despise being called Matilda. I let my family get away with it sometimes. But never ever, under any circumstances, call me that. Mattie is fine. Tildie will do. But if you call me Matilda, life as you now know it will cease to exist."

"Tilde?" He stepped back so that she could pull the leftovers from the refrigerator. "That funny little sideways squiggle used in words to indicate nasality? Or in logic and mathematics to show negation?"

She was pulling two leftover dishes out, but stopped to shoot him an impatient glance. "I thought you had more to do at work."

"How's that?"

"You must have a lot of time on your hands if you can remember such useless, insignificant information. How do you do it?"

"It's a gift," he said with a shrug. "But I could ask

you the same thing. How do *you* do it? Training horses is a lot of work.''

She thought about that as she took two plates and put meat, potatoes, gravy and string beans on them, then put them in the microwave to warm. Then she turned to look at him. "I can't explain it. I just love animals—especially horses. I study their body language and mentally file away their disposition and character. They have traits, you know. Just like people.''

"So you sort of do what I do. Tuck information away in your head. Some of it useless, some of it not,'' he said.

Damn the man. He had her there. Aunt Lily was right. Pride did indeed go before a fall. Her mother was right. She should behave like a lady and be gracious. She would eat a lot less crow that way.

"I guess you're right,'' she said as sweetly as possible. "But you've had so many more years than I've had to gather information. How do you remember it all?''

He folded his arms over his chest. A very impressive chest, she noted with a small surprising flutter of her heart.

"A world-class memory,'' he said, one corner of his mouth lifting. "And fortunately, I'm not ready to take up residence in the geriatric ward yet.''

"I'm sorry. I didn't mean it that way. It's just that what you do boggles the mind. I've never been very good with numbers myself. I'm in awe of anyone who can make sense of it.''

"A lot of what I do is guesswork and instinct. Just like you,'' he said.

She grinned. "But I bet your numbers don't give you love and affection like my horses do."

He laughed. "You win that round. But I have no emotional investment in my numbers the way you do your horses. They can't break my heart."

She saw a black look in his eyes. A remembered pain? She would have sworn that's what it was, and in spite of who he was and how he tweaked her temper, she did feel sorry for him.

"Who broke your heart?" she asked, automatically softening her tone as if she were working with one of the horses.

Instantly the vulnerable expression was gone, replaced by a teasing grin. "What makes you think someone broke my heart?"

"Mother says a person doesn't get through life without some heartbreak. And you've lived so very, very long," she said teasingly. "Surely there are skeletons in your closet."

"Only on Halloween."

"Isn't there a saying in your country—no pain, no gain?"

"I think I've heard that one." He shrugged. "Either I'm emotionally backward, or I've managed to gain without the pain part. What about you? Was your mother right? Have you had your heartbreak in the year-and-a-half you've been on this earth?"

"Cute. I'm not that young." What she was was inexperienced, thanks to her brothers. Except for one single, painful episode. But a stampede of determined Texas mustangs couldn't force her to share the details of that humiliation with him.

"From where I'm standing, you look hardly more than a baby."

Her back started to rise at his comment, making her want to show him that she was a full-grown woman. Her next thought was that he'd turned the conversation away from himself and back to her. Interesting. The words were spoken in a joking manner, but she sensed currents of emotion in him. *Had* someone broken his heart? Or was his pain from something else? She instinctively knew that if she asked, he would put her off.

Instead she watched him, mostly his eyes, then noted the tension in his square jaw. Noted also that he was a very good-looking man, in an older, businessman sort of way. Her heart began to beat very fast, and she grew warm all over. She hadn't felt this way but once, when she *had been* hardly more than a baby. Barely sixteen, she'd managed to elude her brothers long enough to develop a crush on a boy. The incident was a disaster.

But Dawson was a man—the first she'd ever been alone with as a woman. Surely that was the reason her body responded this way when she was near him. That, and the fact that she was *ready* to become a woman in every way. She'd been ready for a long time, but she had way too many brothers who took turns never letting their guard down. The explanation for her reaction to this man had to be that simple. Because Mr. Prescott was absolutely not her type.

But one thought struck her above everything else: her uncle Ryan's comment about his "dynamite" employees. She had a feeling that if she wasn't careful, this particular very male employee could light her fuse and blow up her whole world.

TWO

Dawson helped Mattie set silverware and napkins on the table. When the microwave signaled that the food was warm, she grabbed a pot holder and took the plates to the table. They sat down at a right angle to each other, and she began to shovel food into her mouth as if she hadn't eaten for a month.

"Where's the fire?" he asked.

"Pardon?" she answered. Her gray eyes—very pretty eyes he couldn't help noticing—met his gaze. Then she resumed eating.

"You're going to have indigestion if you don't slow down."

"No worries. I've got the constitution of an elephant."

Not exactly the way he would describe her, Dawson thought ruefully. Those legs. He would bet every last penny of his considerable annual bonus that her gams were not thick and wrinkled and gray. If they were, he was sure the knot in his gut would disappear. Considering the size of that knot, he had a heck of a nerve warning her about indigestion. Or anything else for that matter.

He wished he'd never agreed to keep an eye on her. Even Ryan had questioned his excuse for dropping over tonight, but it was the best he could come up with. He had to be here to watch her. Long-distance baby-sitting wouldn't cut it—Dawson didn't do anything halfway. Besides, just before he'd left, Griff had reminded him that Clint Lockhart was still loose. He had escaped from prison and eluded all law enforcement efforts. The man had sworn revenge on the Fortunes, and was slippery as an eel. He'd already killed Ryan's second wife Sophia—who knew what he might do next?

Dawson knew that being a Fortune made Mattie vulnerable to Clint. If anything happened to her because Dawson slacked off, he wouldn't want to face her brother. But more important, he would never forgive himself.

Suddenly Mattie put her fork down, apparently finished. She stared at him. "Are you one of those anal-retentive people who chew each bite of food twenty-seven times?"

"No," he said, staring at her. "But I don't swallow it whole, either."

"Wouldn't have figured you for a slow eater. You strike me as the kind of man who has places to go, women to meet etcetera, etcetera."

"Nope."

"Really?" She nervously tapped her fingers on the table. "So no one is waiting for you at home?"

"Nope. I'm all yours."

"Until you finish your dinner." She rolled her eyes and heaved a huge sigh before glancing at the clock on the stove. She frowned. "You want to hurry it up?"

He looked at his watch. Eight o'clock. He got the feeling she was in a rush. "You going somewhere?"

"No," she said with a breezy nonchalance that screamed liar. "But it's getting late. I've heard if you

eat too much too late at night, you'll have nightmares.
Your body can turn on you if you make it digest all
that food when it's supposed to be resting. Especially
when you're advanced in years. So if I were you, I'd
quit eating before you regret it.''

Since when did she care about his digestion? Not
only that, but she was as nervous as a long-tailed cat
in a room full of rocking chairs. What the heck was
she up to? ''Come clean, Mattie. Tell me what's going
on.''

Before she could answer, Lily Fortune walked into
the kitchen.

Dawson envied Ryan. Lily was a lovely woman,
and Dawson was glad the two had rekindled their love,
which had begun when they were teenagers.

''I'm sorry to interrupt,'' she said.

''No worries,'' Mattie answered.

''You're not interrupting,'' Dawson said at the same
time.

The older woman smiled at him, then Mattie. ''I
just wanted to let you know that Willa's already gone
upstairs, and Ryan and I are going to make an early
night of it, too. But please make yourselves at home.''

Dawson nodded. ''Thanks.''

''One more thing.'' Lily looked from Dawson to his
fidgety dinner companion. ''Mattie, I just remembered
something.''

''Yes?''

''Tomorrow a group of schoolchildren are coming
to the ranch on a field trip. I think the principal said
they were eleven or twelve years old. They won a
contest, and their prize is a day of horseback riding
on the Double Crown.''

"Can't think of a better reward," Mattie answered enthusiastically.

"I have a favor to ask you. Would you supervise choosing horses for the children? You have such a way with the animals, and the kids couldn't be in better hands than yours."

A sweet smile transformed Mattie's face, making her eyes glow. "I would be happy to, Aunt Lily."

The older woman nodded approvingly. "I understand there will be four or five children. It might be best if you have one of the ranch hands assist you."

The glow in Mattie's eyes turned to a gleam that Dawson didn't trust. He remembered Griff's warning that she was looking to run off with one of the cowboys. Although she'd been working with them on the ranch for some time, Lily had just reminded him how closely. Because of his promise, it was now his problem. He could only think of one solution.

Before opening his mouth, his last thought was that this must be what it felt like to jump out of a skydiving plane. Then he said, "I would be happy to help her."

Mattie, just sipping water, started to cough. Lily patted her on the back. "Are you all right, dear?"

Still coughing, Mattie nodded. Then she stared at him and asked, "You?"

"No, Mel Gibson," he said, hoping to pull this off with humor. "Of course me."

He would have to take the day off. But he'd been working a lot of hours lately, bringing Brody up to snuff on Fortune financial affairs. Dawson had earned himself a comp day. He was meeting Brody at the office in the afternoon. But he could use the morning for baby-sitting detail. To keep her away from the cowboys, he would stick to her like lint to tape.

"Really, that's awfully nice of you." Mattie shot him a look that made a lie of her words. It told him she wished the earth would open and swallow him up. "But one of the ranch hands would probably be more helpful."

"Not necessarily. I've spent a lot of time riding with Zane. I can handle horseback riding basics for kids."

"You don't need me to work that out," Lily said. "I'll say good-night now." She smiled at each of them. "Sleep well, you two."

When they were alone again, Mattie said too sweetly, "Don't you have some numbers to crunch tomorrow? Some minutiae to commit to memory?"

"It can wait."

"You're very generous to offer assistance. But I was thinking of asking Ethan McKenzie."

She'd sure picked someone quick. Maybe she'd had him on her mind all along. For something of a romantic nature? Or an elopement? He couldn't help wondering if Griff was right about her determination to run off with a cowboy. Had she already culled one from the herd, so to speak? All the more reason for Dawson to hang around. Although he had a sneaking suspicion that if he tried to cut the cowboy out completely, she would become even more determined to have him. Not only that, but it could push Dawson into a situation that would tip his hand, and she would figure out that he had promised Griff he'd guard her.

As long as Dawson was around to supervise, he didn't much care who the unfortunate cowboy helper was. "Okay, ask Ethan. But with that many kids, you can probably use more help."

"Probably." She nodded. "Kids can try your patience. They're pretty unpredictable."

"Then you won't mind if I hang around, too."

She looked at him as if he had just said he planned to walk naked from San Antonio to Houston. "Very sporting of you. But I think Ethan and I can handle them. After all, we're both still limber, and practically children ourselves."

"True. An oldtimer like myself has brittle bones. I have to be careful not to break anything. But hasn't anyone ever told you there's no substitute for wisdom and experience?"

"I've heard that. I've seen you riding here on the ranch. But what experience have you had with children?"

"Not much, I'll admit."

"Then give me three good reasons why you would volunteer to put yourself in harm's way with them," she said suspiciously.

"One, maybe it's about time I tried interacting with them. Two, I could be an uncle soon, and kids are still a real mystery to me. And reason number three—if I hang out with kids, maybe I can figure out what makes you tick," he said, watching her face and waiting for the sparks to fly. He wasn't disappointed.

Her gray eyes darkened with something that wasn't quite anger, but was damn defensive. Or maybe it was a defense mechanism. "And why, pray tell, would you want to get to know me better?"

"Beats the heck out of me," he said. "But I do."

Oddly enough, he found that he *did* want to get to know her better. Something about her intrigued him. Her pride. An indomitable spirit that came through loud and clear. She was barely a woman, but he sensed a strength of character beyond her years.

She met his gaze for several moments, gauging him. Finally she said, "I have to give you points for honesty, Mr. Prescott."

"Dawson, please. I feel old enough without you making me feel like my father."

He winced at his own words. After the thoughts he'd had about her, he was hovering way too close to his father's shortcomings as it was.

"All right, Dawson. It's your funeral. But I would appreciate an extra pair of hands. Thanks," she said grinning.

"You're welcome, I think."

She stood. "I'll say good-night then."

"Yeah. I guess it's about that time."

"Oh? And what time would that be?" she asked, the doubtful note in her voice causing her friendly smile to waver.

"Curfew," he answered.

The words produced exactly the effect he'd intended. Her shoulders stiffened, her gray eyes narrowed and finally her full lips thinned. Oddly, he found himself longing to have her sunny smile back.

"I didn't have a curfew even when I should have," she snapped.

"Then what's your hurry? And don't insult my intelligence by saying 'nothing.'"

She peeked over her shoulder as if she were trying to elude surveillance. Then she met his gaze and sighed. "All right. Griff is gone. I suppose it can't do any harm to tell you. It's poker night."

Her brother was right. If she'd known he was a stand-in bodyguard, she would have shut down tighter than a convent school when the fleet was in. "Would you like to expand that explanation a tad?" he asked.

"The ranch hands play poker one evening a week. Tonight's the night. It's an open game. Anyone's invited. I've been dying to learn, but Griff would never let me go. Now's my chance."

"To learn the game?" he asked suspiciously.

"Yes. And get to know the guys better."

"Guys like Ethan McKenzie?"

"Yes."

"The game is open?" When she nodded, he said, "Then no one will mind if I tag along."

He started to walk past her, and she grabbed his arm. "Not so fast, buster. Someone will darn well mind."

"Who?" he asked innocently.

"For starters, me. Why would you want to play poker with a bunch of cowboys? I bet not one of them knows what a tilde is."

"Could be I just want to play poker."

"Yeah, and it could be I'm a high-priced fashion model," she said sarcastically. "Why in the world would you want to spend the evening with a bunch of ranch hands?"

"Like I said before, we haven't had a chance to get to know each other since you've been here. This is as good a time as any."

"For whom?" she asked.

"For me. After all, if I'm going to help you with the kids tomorrow, it seems to me that we would be a more efficient team if we knew each other better."

"We're not a team."

"We will be."

"When snowballs survive in hell," she said.

He ignored her remark and said wistfully, "It's been a long time since I've played poker."

"Why?" She tipped her head to the side and studied him. "Don't you have any friends of your own?"

"Of course I have friends. What would make you ask that?"

"Now that Zane and Gwen are married, you must be pretty lonesome." She gave him an impertinent look.

She thought he needed to make friends? She actually thought Zane Fortune was his only friend? She couldn't genuinely believe that he had no one to hang out with. He cringed at the idea. When Griff got back, they were going to have a long talk about indebtedness. This favor was getting more complicated all the time.

And on top of her zingers, she was actually starting to appeal to him.

"No, I'm not lonesome. I have my spreadsheets to keep me warm," he said. Not to mention thoughts of her long legs…. That image made him hot all over. "I just like to play cards. Okay?" he asked more abrasively than he had intended.

"Even if I'm there?"

Especially if you're there and your brother isn't, he thought. "How can you ask that?" Before she could answer he took her arm and said, "Let's go, Mattie. Seven card stud awaits."

"Huh?"

"No worries," he said, imitating her. "You'll find out."

But he didn't miss the gleam in her eyes at the word *stud.*

* * *

The ranch hands lived in a bunkhouse about three-quarters of a mile from the main house. With Griff around, she'd never had a chance to see the inside. But she'd heard the guys talking, and knew it was Ethan and Bobby Lee's turn to host tonight's poker game. Mattie wanted to jump into the truck she used to get herself around the ranch, but Dawson insisted on walking. It seemed odd to her, since there was a chill November wind blowing. But then, it seemed odd that he was with her at all.

She'd been half joking when she'd said it, but maybe he really *didn't* have any friends. That, along with the fact that he was cooped up inside far too much, pushing around all those numbers, made her feel kind of sorry for him. It could explain why he wanted to hoof it to the bunkhouse. He must have a fresh air deficiency.

It wasn't easy keeping up with his long stride. She was slightly winded by the time they stepped onto the wooden bunkhouse porch. Low voices drifted to them from inside. Now that she was here, Mattie was a little nervous. She was almost grateful that Dawson was with her so she didn't have to walk in alone. It was a bit like going to a school dance with one of her brothers, except that Dawson Prescott would mind his own business and not hers once they were inside. Anticipation chased away her nerves.

She was about to knock, then glanced at him. The light next to the door picked up the angles of his face, making it look rugged and very masculine. And quite attractive. Her heart gave a strange little lurch. When she spoke, her voice was slightly breathless. From their sprint over here, no doubt, she thought. Because she couldn't believe that he was starting to look good to her.

"You don't have to do this if you're tired," she told him.

"On the contrary. I'm looking forward to it." He looked at her uncertainly. "I should warn you about something."

"What?" she asked.

"Cowboys don't like to play cards with a woman."

She gaped at him for a moment, then shook her head. "Surely you can do better than that, Dawson."

He was trying to talk her out of playing. Why? More importantly, why had he suddenly agreed to accompany her? She'd been on the Double Crown for several months, and they'd had little contact. When he'd first suggested coming with her to the game, she'd wondered if, possibly, he was intimidated by Griff and was taking advantage of the fact that her brother was gone to hang out with her. Now she knew she'd been wrong. He was trying to get rid of her. But Matilda Fortune didn't scare easy.

"Seriously, Mattie. Cowboys are superstitious. They think it's bad luck to deal a woman in."

"Then why did they invite me?" She tried to keep her voice level and pleasant. Not easy when she wanted to bop him.

"They're superstitious *and* polite."

"I'm willing to risk it."

"It's your funeral," he said. He shrugged and stuck his hands in his pockets, lifting his suit jacket.

It was a blatantly masculine pose in spite of his sissy suit. That made her wonder what he would look like dressed in jeans and boots, like a cowboy. She had a feeling the image would give her no peace of mind.

"Okay," she answered with an emphatic nod, then rapped on the door.

"Come in." That was Bobby Lee's voice.

Mattie turned the knob and pushed the door inward. She was surprised to see that only three cowboys were there. Ethan and Bobby Lee who shared the cabin, and Burch Picket, a hand who had been hired around the time she'd arrived. They looked up from their cards when Mattie walked in.

She had a quick impression of wooden floors and several bunks. In the corner, there were couches and a couple of chairs in front of a television. The other corner held a small kitchen complete with refrigerator and stove. There was an empty space in the middle because they'd pulled the table into the cabin's main room for the game.

Her gaze rested on dark-haired, brown-eyed Ethan. She knew he was right around her own age, but he looked about seventeen. Even his sunburned face didn't hide the fact that he'd hardly started shaving yet. She thought he was cute, but was vaguely disturbed that being in the same room with him didn't produce any sort of physical response on her part. Not the way being around Dawson did. But that probably had something to do with how angry she'd been the first time she met him, and how he baited her every time he opened his mouth. Ethan seemed like a sweetie, and she just had to get to know him better.

"Hi, guys," she said, greeting all the men.

"What are you doing here, Mattie?" Bobby Lee didn't look too happy. The blond, blue-eyed cowboy's frown was a big clue.

Her heart fell. That wasn't exactly the greeting she'd been hoping for. "It's poker night," she said lamely.

"Yeah." Ethan threw his cards down. "But we didn't think you would—"

"Howdy, stranger." Bobby Lee smiled slowly and stood up, walking toward her. "Been a long time."

"Not that long," she said, confused.

Then she shivered as she felt *him* behind her. She'd momentarily forgotten. *Dawson*. He was so close, and the heat of his body warmed her clear down to her toes. The scent of his cologne tied her stomach in knots. Her heart skipped a beat, kicking her confusion up a notch.

"Yeah, it has been a long time," Dawson answered, reaching out to shake hands with him.

Ethan joined them, just inside the door. "Good to see you," the young cowboy said.

"Goes for me, too. We haven't seen much of you since Zane got married and you quit hanging out here with him." Bobby Lee chimed in. "Dawson, you know Burch Pickett, right?"

"We've met," he said.

The man nodded. "Howdy."

"Ethan, pull up a chair for Dawson."

"What about me?" Mattie asked, hands on her hips.

"Oh, Mattie," Bobby Lee said. There was less warmth in his voice than when he'd greeted Dawson. "I figured you just brought Dawson down here to be neighborly. You're really fixin' t'play cards, are you?"

"That was my plan." She felt about as welcome as the plague.

Ethan pulled over another chair and put it next to

the first. "Here you go, Mattie," he said. "Take a load off, Dawson."

They sat next to each other at the round table, at the center of which sat a bowl of popcorn and another of pretzels. Cards, coins and bills were scattered across the scratched wooden top.

While the men were moving around getting drinks and refilling snack bowls, she whispered to Dawson, "Do you know what the money is for?"

"Betting," he said. "Makes it more interesting."

She would have to take his word on that. She had a bigger problem. "I don't have any money with me. Do you?"

He looked at her as if she had pink hair. "Of course I've got money."

"Can you lend me some? Just until we get back to the house?"

"Okay." He pulled out some folded bills and handed her a couple as he asked, "Do you know anything about poker?"

"Nope. But how hard can it be?" she asked, taking the money.

Ethan handed Dawson a beer and said, "You deal."

"Where's my beer?" Mattie asked, anxious to be a part of the whole thing, to experience everything.

"Are you old enough to drink?" Dawson asked, a twinkle in his eyes. "I'd ask for ID if I were you," he said to Ethan.

"Number one, I'm twenty-one," she said. "Number two, thanks to you, we're on foot and not driving. So who cares if I have a beer?" It annoyed her no end that none of the cowboys moved until Dawson gave them a nod.

"Thanks," she said, when Ethan set the beer can in

front of her. She looked at Dawson. "Now you can deal."

"All right, your ladyship." He looked around at the chuckling men, then his gaze rested on her. She didn't miss the challenge there. With supreme confidence he began shuffling the deck. "Mattie has never played before." The remark produced a series of black looks and barely concealed annoyance. "So let's start with something simple."

That was the Dawson she'd come to know and *not* love. He didn't have to do her any favors. She made a mental note to give him a piece of her mind later. "No need to go easy on me," she said. "I'll pick it up fast."

He smiled, irritating her with the genuine cheerfulness in his look. "All right," he said. "No special treatment." He started to deal, letting the cards land facedown in front of each player. "How about seven card, no peek, roll your own, one-eyed jacks and kings with mustaches wild?" he asked.

Mattie stared at him. "Roll your own? Is this cigarettes or poker?"

"Poker. Do you want me to deal you out?"

"Not on your life," she said, sipping her beer. *Nasty stuff,* she thought. But she would drink the whole can and ask for another before she would let one of them know how much she hated it. "I just have one question. What's this about one-eyed jacks and kings with mustaches?"

Dawson stopped dealing, and quickly riffled through the deck, pulling out the cards in question. He showed her the difference. She nodded. "Thanks," she said. "You can finish now."

He buried the cards to everyone's satisfaction and

completed the job. Without a word, Ethan, who sat on Dawson's right, flipped over his top card. It was a nine of clubs. Then he tossed a dollar into the center of the table. When everyone did the same, she put money in, too. Burch turned over four of his cards, and stopped when he showed a king—clean-shaven, Mattie noticed. He put three dollars on the table, and everyone else did, too. This could get expensive, she thought.

Next Bobby Lee started turning over cards. Since none of them had picked up all their cards, she figured out what "no peek" meant. Then it was her turn. She flipped over four cards before she turned over an ace. She leaned over to Dawson and whispered, "What do I do now?"

"Bet," he answered.

"On what?" she asked.

"You have the highest card showing."

"So I win?" She looked at him.

"Not until all the cards are turned over and we see who has the best hand."

"What's a hand?" She ignored the groans and sighs from the other men.

Dawson patiently explained. "In poker there are hands—a pair, two pair, three of a kind, full house, etcetera up to the highest, which is a royal flush."

She looked down at the table again. "It seems sort of foolish to put money out not knowing if I can win."

"That's part of the fun," he said. "But if you don't want to bet, just say 'check.'"

"Check," she answered.

Dawson turned over all his cards and apparently had nothing, because he said, "I'm out."

They went around the table again. Burch had two kings and two threes—"two pair," someone said.

When it was her turn, she flipped over all her cards and was excited when she saw three aces. All the men groaned.

She looked at Dawson. "Is this good?"

"Yeah. You win," he said. "All the money is yours."

"Really?" This was very exciting. No wonder they did it once a week. She scooped up the bills and coins from the center of the table and returned the money she'd borrowed from Dawson. "Who deals next?" she asked.

Ethan picked up the cards and dealt them. The game moved a bit faster, until Dawson had to explain to her again what constituted a hand and what beat what. There was so much groaning in the room, it sounded like a haunted house on Halloween. And when she won the second round, she felt guilty, and tried not to take the pot. But they insisted, albeit angrily. "Beginner's luck," one of them grumbled.

"Now who deals?" she asked.

Bobby Lee yawned. "It's gettin' pretty late."

Mattie glanced at the clock. It was only nine-fifteen.

Burch stood up. "I gotta get goin'. See y'all later." Faster than you could say "lickety-split," he was gone.

Ethan yawned again and said, "I have to be up early."

"Me, too," Bobby Lee said.

Mattie was confused, a state of mind that was becoming increasingly familiar to her the more time she spent in the company of men who were *not* her brothers. From all she'd heard, these games went on until the wee hours. This seemed very early to break up. And she had just been getting the hang of it. Was

Dawson right about the guys feeling that she was bad luck? Or were they miffed because she had all the *good luck?* Poor sports! She almost blurted that out, but decided against it.

"Guess we'd better go and let these guys get some shut-eye," Dawson said. He curved his hand around her arm and pulled her to a standing position with him.

She noticed that Ethan didn't waste any time opening the door. The chill wind blew in, but it wasn't as cold as the room had been when she'd raked in the last pot. Still, she figured she could be gracious and not let on that she knew they were upset because she'd won. Having so many brothers had taught her a lot about male pride.

"You're right. I have to get up early, too," she said, making her way to the door. "I almost forgot. Aunt Lily asked me to supervise some schoolchildren who are coming to the ranch tomorrow. She suggested that I pick someone to help me with them. How about it, Ethan?" she asked, looking up at him. He was tall and lanky. Not unattractive, but not muscular like Dawson....

She wondered where that thought had come from. It was followed quickly by a fervent hope that this sudden hang-up she'd developed of comparing all men to Dawson Prescott was something she'd get over soon.

"Sure, Mattie," Ethan said. "I'll give you a hand. If Mrs. Fortune wants me to," he answered.

"Good," she said. "I'll see you in the corral around nine-thirty." She thought Dawson mumbled something. "What did you say?"

"I said, let's go and let these guys get some sleep."

Dawson took her elbow none too gently and guided her off the porch.

They started walking toward the big house. Mattie was vaguely disturbed at the abrupt way the evening had ended. Since Dawson had witnessed everything, she decided to risk asking him. "Did it seem to you that the guys were bad sports?"

In the moonlight, she read the wry look he gave her. "Why do you say that?"

"Because I've been around long enough to see them drag to work after a late night of poker. They don't let an early-morning wake-up call stop them—if they're winning. Do you think they were upset because I had some beginner's luck?"

He shook his head. "Nope. It's the female thing."

She stared at him. "Define 'female thing.'"

"Bad luck to play cards with a girl."

"Then why deal me in at all? Or why mention the game in front of me?"

He shrugged. "You're the boss's niece. They couldn't very well tell you to go home."

"I just wish they'd been honest."

Their shoulders happened to brush at that moment and she felt him flinch—or abruptly pull away from the contact. She wasn't sure which. Before she could puzzle it out, they arrived at her front door.

This was the first time a man had ever escorted her home. That thought produced a nervous sort of feeling in the pit of her stomach. But this was Dawson.

"If I'm bad luck, then you won't want to help me with the kids tomorrow."

"I'll risk it," he said. "An honorable man doesn't go back on a promise."

"Suit yourself," she said and went inside.

She leaned against the door and thought again about how Dawson reminded her of dynamite. The more time she spent in his company, the closer the match got to her fuse.

Three

The next morning, Dawson leaned against the corral fence and watched Mattie walk toward him, up the slight hill, from the house. She was surrounded by four kids—a girl and three boys. He wondered what the sassy Aussie would say when he told her Ethan wouldn't be joining them. After clearing it with Lily Fortune, he had volunteered his services so that the young cowboy could better use his time on another chore. Oddly enough, he had derived great satisfaction from taking Ethan out of the equation, but wasn't exactly sure why.

Ditto on the fact that he was anticipating Mattie's explosive reaction to the news. That's what a woman did when her plans didn't pan out. He'd learned that the hard way. He'd been raised by a mother who'd been dumped for a younger woman, so bad news had been abundant. His mother had become increasingly depressed and bitter—a natural reaction when the man she loved had married an adolescent.

It made him determined not to use any woman and then throw her away. It had also taught him skills to deal with an unhappy female. So he had no qualms about giving Mattie the bad news about Ethan. But before he fired the first salvo for World War III, he enjoyed the sway of her hips and her graceful long-legged stride. He noticed the sparkle in her gray eyes and heard her merry laughter after she bent her head and listened to one of the boys. Dawson remembered Griff saying that she'd never met a stranger. He could see the evidence for himself. She'd just met these kids, and she had them eating out of her hand.

He knew that wouldn't be happening if she didn't like kids. And he recalled the other thing Griff had warned him about: she wanted to have a baby. Soon. No matter how ticked she was that he'd canceled out Ethan, it couldn't be as bad as her brother's reaction if she ran away with the wet-behind-the-ears cowboy.

Mattie spotted him and stumbled slightly. Then the group continued on until she and her cowboy wannabes stood in a semicircle around him. The kids gave him odd looks, as if they'd been warned about him. She gave him an appraising glance. *Saucy.* The word described perfectly the way she was eyeing him. And it made him feel like he was a prize quarter horse ready to be put to stud.

Two could play that game. "Something wrong, your ladyship?" he asked, lifting one eyebrow.

"You tell me. Who are you and what have you done with Dawson Prescott?"

He looked down at his scuffed brown boots, worn jeans, and long-sleeved, white cotton shirt. "What's wrong?"

"For starters, you're not wearing your uniform. Where's the white dress shirt, pin-striped suit, red power tie, and loafers with tassels?"

"First of all, I draw the line at loafers with a tassel. Too froufrou. As for the rest, it's hanging in the closet at home in Kingston Estates."

"Ah." She nodded. "The large planned community in San Antonio for the fabulously wealthy."

"You make it sound like a communicable disease."

"If only it were," she sighed.

He glanced down at his boots. "I repeat, is there something wrong?"

"You just look different this way."

"Different good? Or different bad?"

"Different as in less like a stuffed shirt."

"Well, thank you, I think, your ladyship," he said dryly.

She thought he was a stuffed shirt? If he wasn't on assignment for Griff Fortune, he'd show her a thing or two about stuffed shirts. But the fact was that he was here to fend off the other guys, not to teach her anything about men.

She looked around. "I wonder where Ethan is. It's almost ten. I did tell him nine-thirty."

"Actually you told him *around* nine-thirty. I talked to the foreman. He said he needed him for a job. Since I'm here to assist you with your charges, it didn't seem necessary to replace him." He glanced at the kids. The boys were eyeing him as if he had just torched their baseball card collection, and the little girl openly stared at him as if he walked on water. "I'm your only backup."

"That's too bad," she said. "I was looking forward to spending some time with him."

He felt only a slight twinge of guilt for his part in producing her disappointed look. At least, he thought it was guilt. It couldn't be jealousy. He wasn't interested in Mattie that way. Even if she were his type, she was too young. All he cared about was fulfilling his promise to her brother and getting himself off baby-sitting detail. If she found the cowboy type she was looking for, it wouldn't be on his watch.

But her reaction surprised him. Disappointment was a far cry from the explosion he'd expected. He wasn't sure if that was good or bad.

And it didn't much matter. If they got this show on the road pronto, maybe he could get in a couple of hours at the office later.

"So where do we start?" he asked.

"How about introductions." She looked around at the kids and her gaze rested on the small redheaded girl with cornflower-blue eyes. "Ladies first. Katie Mansfield, meet Dawson Prescott."

He held his hand out and the girl, who looked about eleven years old, put hers into his palm, squeezing with a surprising strength. "Miss Mansfield, it's a pleasure to meet you."

"And this motley macho male crew are Nate Howe, Juan Castaneda, and Kevin Dolan." She pointed to a tall, skinny blonde, then a husky dark-haired, black-eyed boy and a chubby guy with unruly brown hair. The boys appeared to be about the same age as Katie.

One by one, they shook hands with Dawson. "It's nice to meet you," he said.

"Now we need to find you just the right mounts," Mattie said. "C'mon, mates."

She lead the way toward the barn, and Dawson's gaze was pulled to the feminine grace of her walk. The hem of her plaid shirt hitched up a notch, and he got a better look at her curvy rear end. He couldn't help wondering if she had a small waist and shapely hips to go with those dynamite legs. All the Matilda images he'd been fighting against—legs wrapped around his waist, twisted sheets and bodies entwined—flooded his consciousness with a vengeance.

All those thoughts were at odds with her fresh-scrubbed face and the long blond braid hanging down her back. She was just a kid. And he was her chaperone—not her Casanova. He was abruptly drawn back to the present by a persistent tugging.

"Don't you just love her accent?" Katie asked Dawson. She took his hand and tugged him forward.

"I do," he answered. Oddly enough, he meant it.

Inside the barn, Mattie walked down the hay-strewn aisle between stalls. She looked from side to side, tapping her lips thoughtfully. Stopping beside one, she said, "Juan, this one is for you. His name is Buck." She continued on until she came to a black, beige, and white pinto. "Katie, this is Buttercup. She has a disposition as sweet as yours."

Dawson watched her pick out two more mounts for Kevin and Nate. Then she grabbed a bridle, handed it to him, and said, "Mr. Prescott is going to demonstrate bridling a horse."

She tapped her lip again. "He'll show you on Buttercup. She's very patient, but—" she gave the kids a serious look "—you must be very gentle with the animals. Treat them the way you would like to be treated. You don't like it if someone punches or slaps you. Right?"

Kevin nodded. "Juan and Nate do that to each other all the time when we line up at school."

Mattie glanced at the two who looked guilty. "But you're not going to do that now. Are you, guys?"

"No," they said in unison.

She looked at him. "Mr. Prescott, you're on."

"Dawson." He looked at the kids. "It's all right to call me by my first name."

Mattie met his gaze. "He thinks Mr. Prescott makes him sound old," she said conspiratorially to the kids.

"He *is* old," Nate said.

"Do you think so?" she said, eyeing Dawson critically. "I guess you just have to get to know him. He doesn't look so ancient to me."

Dawson gritted his teeth. He had no problem being gentle with Buttercup, but there was a certain smart-mouthed female who could use a dressing-down. He wasn't ancient. But the part of him that disconnected from his wounded ego acknowledged that the kid was right. Compared to Mattie, he *was* old.

He congratulated himself on controlling his temper, while Mattie led the way as they walked back to the multicolored Buttercup's stall. When they stopped in front of the mare, she looked at the group with sweet, gentle brown eyes. Dawson hated to admit it, but Mattie was right to pick this animal to demonstrate on. Not only that, but being familiar with all the horses in the barn, he knew each one she'd chosen was sweet-natured and pliable. He realized why Lily Fortune had asked her to supervise the schoolkids. Mattie knew her stuff. And she was as good with the kids as she was with horses.

"Okay, listen up, you guys—and ladies," he added. He didn't miss Katie's pleased smile. Too bad his charm didn't work to tame a certain impertinent Australian miss. "I'm going to show you how this is done, but before you try it, there's something you have to do. Anyone have a clue what it is?"

"Get a ladder for Katie?" Juan said to a round of laughter from his friends.

"No." Dawson looked at each one in turn, but they all shrugged and shook their heads. He met Mattie's gaze, and the sparkle in her eyes told him she knew what he had in mind. "Do you want to tell them?" he asked her.

She nodded. "You must get to know the animal before you try to do anything. These horses are used to a lot of different people riding them, and they're okay with that. But not all animals are that way."

"How do we get to know them?" Nate asked Dawson.

"Have you ever heard the expression that the way to a man's heart is through his stomach?" Four pairs of eyes looked back at him blankly. Maybe he was more ancient than he'd thought. When he looked into the fifth pair of eyes, he saw laughter. The merriment made Mattie's eyes very beautiful. The look made him very warm.

"What Dawson means is that you can make friends with the animals by feeding them, gently touching them and talking quietly to them. They respond best to gentle kindness, not fear and intimidation. After he shows you how to bridle Buttercup, I'll show you where the carrots are kept for feeding the horses. But before we do that, I'll show you how it's done so that you don't get your fingers nipped." She smiled sweetly at Dawson. "Please continue, professor."

Oh, good, he thought. Not teacher, but professor. She just had to make him feel that much older. He spread the leather strips so that they could see the configuration and how it would fit around the horse's face.

"This metal part, called a bit, goes in the horse's mouth. If you haven't made friends with the horse, no way will the animal open up willingly. Consequently, no way will you get it in. Observe." He patted the horse's neck and crooned to her. Then he put the bit in front of her, and she opened her mouth. He used his palm to push it until she allowed it to settle behind her teeth. "Voilà," he said.

Kevin scratched his head, which didn't do his unruly brown hair any favor. "What does walla mean?"

"It means he did it easy as pie," Mattie explained. "Did you notice the way Dawson pushed the bit in with his palm? He kept his fingers out of the way. Horses can get confused and bite. They don't mean to hurt you, but it can happen if you're not careful."

"You mean accidentally?" Katie asked.

"Exactly," Mattie answered, as if the little girl were a star pupil. She moved to the other side of the horse and glanced at Dawson. He thought there was approval in her eyes. Obviously she was surprised that he'd passed her bridle test. He knew that's why she'd asked him to show the kids how it was done. He was glad he'd favorably surprised her.

Mattie patted Buttercup's neck. "For safety purposes, when you give them carrots, keep your palm flat and your fingers out of the way. Buttercup would feel awful if she hurt you."

"How do you know that?" Juan asked.

"I can see it in her eyes." She hugged the horse for a few seconds. "All right. Dawson, you take Katie and Juan. I'll take Kevin and Nate, and we'll get the horses bridled and saddled. Meet you in the corral."

"Right," he said.

About twenty minutes later, they were gathered in the picket-fenced enclosure. All four kids were mounted on their horses.

"Giddyap, horse," Kevin said, moving his body in a forward motion.

"Hold on, buckaroo. I need to adjust your stirrups." Mattie smiled up at the young boy sitting on the horse.

''You need to stick your feet in there. If they flap around like wet noodles, it could scare the horse. If the horse is scared, she might run away with you. If she runs away with you, you'll be scared. If you're scared, I'm scared. If—''

''Okay, Mattie,'' Kevin grinned. ''I get it. I'll hold my horse while you fix the stirrups.''

''Good choice. All of you hold your horses until Dawson and I make sure the stirrups are adjusted to fit you. Okay?''

''No worries,'' they said together.

She laughed, and Dawson grinned, too, watching her. She was wonderful with them. Patient and reasonable. The kids responded in kind. Why was she so *un*reasonable when it came to him?

When everyone was secure, Dawson saddled a horse for himself and one for Mattie. He led them into the corral, where she watched and instructed as the four rode slowly around the perimeter. She and Dawson mounted up.

''All right, kids. I think you're ready. We're going to see how you do out in the open. This is going to be an adventure.''

''Truer words have never been spoken,'' Dawson muttered, watching her trim back as he followed her out of the corral.

''Jillian, I can't thank you enough for coming with me.''

''It's my pleasure to show you the sights of San Antonio.'' Jillian tucked a strand of straight blond hair behind her ear.

Mattie smiled at her soon-to-be sister-in-law across the table. It was hard to believe just that morning she'd been teaching kids to ride in the wide-open spaces of Texas. And now, eight hours later, she was taking in the newest "in club" in San Antonio. She turned her head from side to side, trying to see everything at once.

She noticed the sawdust-covered floor, saloon-style bar, and old-fashioned Western lanterns sitting on the round tables. Anticipation hummed through her. The most impressive sight was the multitude of men bellied up to the bar, boots hooked on the stools.

"So this is the famous Watering Hole, bar and nightspot extraordinaire," she said.

"This is it." Jillian shifted uncomfortably on the wooden, barrel-backed chair. "This is where single women come to meet single men—cowboys hang out here in…droves, so to speak."

"I already noticed the cowboys. It's so exciting. And about time, thanks to my brothers. I feel as if I've missed out on so much. Maybe I can see a little big-city nightlife without my shadow hovering over me."

"You shouldn't be so hard on Griff, Mattie. He loves you and is trying to protect you."

"I know he means well. They all do. But there are so many of them. I thought when I came to Texas, I would have the freedom of a single woman. But every time I turn around, I trip over one of the Fortune boys. Why can't they just let me live my life?"

"Maybe if I'd had a big brother watching over me, I wouldn't have made so many mistakes." Jillian sighed, a big, gusty, sad sound.

Mattie felt guilty and ungrateful for complaining. Truthfully, she didn't know what she would do if anything happened to one of her brothers. Impulsively, she reached across the table and squeezed the other woman's hand. She envied Jillian Hart Tanner's petite, pretty, blond good looks. Next to her, Mattie felt like a galumphing elephant. But she genuinely liked Jillian, and envied her happiness and the baby that would soon arrive for her and Brody.

"Things will be fine for you, Jillian. God knows why you want him—" she grinned "—but you've got my brother now. Soon you'll be married, and he'll take good care of you and the baby." Her gaze dropped to the other woman's gently rounded abdomen, and a sigh escaped. "I envy you so. I'd like to have children. If only I could find someone to care about me the way Brody does you."

"I've loved him for so many years." Jillian's blue-green eyes always sparkled, but never more than when she mentioned her man. "I truly hope you find someone and are as happy as I am."

"Me, too." She glanced around the room again, checking out the men. She did a double take as she saw a man who looked an awful lot like her brother crossing the room. The man was wearing Brody's frown. Behind him was none other than Dawson Prescott's twin. At least, she hoped it was. She couldn't be so unlucky that the two of them would show up here.

"I don't believe it," she muttered, "How could they have found me here?"

Jillian looked uneasy. "I hope you don't mind. When I went to the ladies' room—the place I spend so much time in these days," she said ruefully, "I called Brody. The corporate office is practically around the corner. I missed him and just wanted to say hello. He was in a meeting with Dawson. I told him where we were and asked him to meet us if he could.''

"Imagine that." Mattie wondered which of the gods she had offended. Why was she being punished?

"I thought they would be at the office much longer," Jillian continued. "He must have dropped everything. For me." She smiled, the expression of a woman in love. "Isn't he wonderful?"

The two men stopped at their table and looked down. Fresh from the office, they were wearing slacks and dress shirts. They stood out like Rockettes with broken legs. Worse, she was disturbed that Dawson looked as good, if not better, than he had just that morning when she'd seen him in jeans and boots. She was afraid even a burlap bag wouldn't hide his muscular frame and the masculinity that made her senses sit up and take notice.

Mattie squirmed under her brother's stare, not so much because she knew he was angry, but because Dawson was there to witness the chewing out she knew was coming. "Hi, bro," she said. "What's going on?"

"That's what I'd like to know, Matilda."

She winced, then glanced at Dawson and didn't miss the expression on his face. He was grinning. Not with his mouth, but she could see it in his eyes. On the inside, he was smiling from ear to ear. Maybe she didn't hate her name as much as the fact that when someone called her Matilda she was usually in trouble. Why, oh, why did Dawson have to be here? He already treated her as if she were twelve years old. Now he was witness to her brother treating her like a twelve-year-old delinquent.

She looked up—way up—and met Brody's gray-eyed gaze. That black hair of his and the stern look on his handsome face might intimidate some people. But not her. Caught she might be, but cornered—never.

She lifted her chin. "I'm checking out San Antonio nightlife, Brody. Your fiancée very kindly agreed to accompany me, since she knows the area."

Brody smiled at Jillian, and a person would have to be blind not to see all the love in his expression. But when he glanced her way again, Mattie squirmed. The grim look was back.

"She's pregnant, Mattie," he said. "What in the world possessed you to drag her to a place like this?"

Jillian put her hand on his arm. "She didn't drag me, Brody. She couldn't. I'm the size of a beached whale—it would take a crane to move me anywhere these days. Don't be so hard on her." Jillian linked her fingers with his. "There's nothing wrong with this place. Besides, I'm pregnant, not sick. Being here won't hurt me." She leaned forward and said, "Hi, Dawson."

He smiled. "Hi, yourself. How are you?"

"Fine, now that you guys are here. I was missing Brody a bunch."

"Can I get you ladies something to drink?" he asked.

When he met her gaze, Mattie noticed that same glint in his eyes, the one that pegged her as an amusing child. How she would love to wipe that look off his face and show him a thing or two about the woman she was.

But now wasn't the time. And since he was here, Mattie decided, he might as well make himself useful. "I'd like a glass of wine," she said.

"Sparkling water for me," Jill chimed in.

Brody glared at Mattie. "Make it two waters," he said to Dawson.

"Sweetheart," Jillian said to him, "why don't you go along with Dawson and help him carry the drinks?"

He bent over to kiss her cheek. "Whatever you say."

When the two men were gone, Mattie didn't miss the pitying look Jillian sent her way. "I'm sorry, Mattie," she said. "I wouldn't have called him if I'd known he would act that way."

"Don't worry about it. At least you're with the man you love and he makes you happy. It's just my bad luck that he acts like a mother hen." What bothered her more was Dawson's presence. He would see her big brother treating her like a kid when she was doing her best to show him she was a grown woman.

Jillian glanced over to the bar where the two men were talking while waiting for the drink order. "Your brother's intentions are good, Mattie."

"Maybe. But you know what they say about the road to hell." Dejectedly, Mattie rested her chin in her hand.

"Just you leave him to me when they come back."

Mattie watched several cowboys move around on a small dais in the corner of the room. Three picked up a couple of guitars and a fiddle, while one sat at a keyboard and another tested the microphone. Then they began to play a slow, country and western song. The words were sad, about love gone bad. Mattie had only one experience with love. Adolescent love—definitely gone bad. But she was willing to give romance another try. How else was she going to find her soul mate and have the family she wanted so badly?

She glanced around the room, attempting to catch the eye of one of the unattached men present. Trying to look available and pleasant, she plastered a smile on her face. No one gave her a second look.

Her small window of opportunity slammed shut when Brody and Dawson returned with the drinks. Her brother sat next to Jillian and possessively draped his arm across her shoulders. She snuggled into him with a contented sigh. Dawson was forced to take the empty chair at the table beside her, and content wasn't exactly the word Mattie would use to describe his body language. In fact, he angled all of his very attractive muscles as far away from her as he could get and still remain in the same county.

But Mattie didn't miss the glances he received from other women in the room. And the realization gave her the strangest feeling, like the weight of a stone sitting on her chest.

"Brody?" Jillian smiled sweetly.

"Hmm?"

"Would you dance with me?"

He gave her rounded belly a skeptical look. "Is it all right? Not too much exertion?"

"I had more exertion last night," she said, smiling seductively at him. He grinned—a look of supreme male satisfaction that Mattie didn't quite understand.

"Okay, lady. Let's do it." He held out his hand, and Jillian put her small one in his palm and let him help her to her feet.

They walked to the dance floor without a backward glance—as if they were the only two people in the world. Mattie watched Brody take Jillian in his arms, and she went willingly, resting her head against his chest. He brushed his cheek across her hair and rubbed his thumb across the back of her hand as they swayed to the music.

Mattie envied them. Would she ever have eyes for just one man and he for her? Would any man ever hold her as if she were the most precious person in his world? As if his life would be meaningless without her? She glanced around the room at all the men who kept to themselves. *Not any time soon,* she thought ruefully.

"You know Brody means well." Dawson met her gaze.

"Jillian said the same thing to me."

"She's right." He took a sip of his beer. "He cares about you."

"She said that, too. And that if she'd had brothers to watch out for her maybe she wouldn't have made mistakes in her life."

"She could be right." Dawson glanced at the couple on the dance floor.

"On the other hand, maybe those mistakes made her appreciate a good thing when she found it. How will I know unless I get a chance to live?" Mattie asked, not really expecting Dawson to answer.

"Patience, Mattie. He'll be married soon. When the baby arrives, he won't have time to keep track of you. And he'll be too tired. I understand babies have this annoying habit of eating every two or three hours, day and night."

"Annoying?" She studied him. "Don't you like kids? After the way you handled them this morning, you could have fooled me."

One corner of his mouth quirked. "Did you just pay me a compliment?"

"No way." But she couldn't help grinning back at him. "You just looked like you were having the time of your life, and the kids took to you like ducks to water. I figured you would want half a dozen."

He shook his head. "It scares the hell out of me. I'm beginning to think stability is a myth. And I wouldn't bring a baby boy into this world without a guarantee of that."

She took a sip from her glass, secretly grateful that it was water. "When my little girl comes into this world, I will welcome her with open arms. Two o'clock feedings and all."

He raised one eyebrow. "Little girl?"

"If you can have a boy, why can't I have a girl?"

He shrugged. "No reason. Especially since the way you handled those schoolkids was damn close to miraculous. I was bowled over at how you sized up each one and picked just the right horse. The whole thing went a lot more smoothly than I would have guessed. Thanks to your expertise."

"Did you just pay me a compliment?" she asked, joking because she didn't know how else to act.

"No way," he said, but the amusement in his eyes belied the words.

His praise made her glow from head to toe. Inside and out. She didn't know nice words from a man could make her feel this way. If only it had been something about how desirable she was, instead of her ability with horses. Then she would see his indifference and raise him a flirtation or two.

"What I did isn't a miracle," she said. "I've always

liked children. And I haven't made a secret of the fact that I would like to have one. Soon.''

He leveled an appraising glance around the room, then met her gaze. ''First you have to grow up, your ladyship.''

Four

"I don't really look like a kid." Mattie looked at Willa and Jillian for confirmation as she pushed her salad around her plate.

It was the day after her night before. Her very unimpressive night before on the town. She was having lunch in San Antonio with her two friends after shopping for bridal dresses for Jillian's wedding. Uncle Ryan's goddaughter had accompanied them. Mattie found her easy to talk to in spite of her recently acquired doctorate in Political Science. She had free time since she wasn't due to start teaching at Texas A & M until the following semester.

After several moments, she realized no one had commented on her statement. "Do I look like a kid?" She saw the glance the two women exchanged. "Tell me the truth."

Jillian took her lemon slice from the rim of her glass and dropped it into her iced tea. "Of course you don't, Mattie."

"If I don't look too young, then I'm a two-bagger," she said.

Willa frowned. "Define 'two-bagger.'"

"I need to wear a bag over my head in public and I'm so grotesque that one isn't enough."

"Don't be ridiculous, Mattie." Jillian skewered a piece of chicken in her salad.

''Then why didn't any of the men in the bar last night approach me?'' Mattie asked, looking at first one then the other of her friends.

After Dawson's remark about her growing up, she had increased her efforts to attract attention. To ditch her brother and sashay through the place by herself, she'd used the excuse of going to the ladies' room. Apparently, she'd done it once too often, because finally Brody had asked if she had a problem. Her only problem was the look of amusement she'd seen on Dawson's face. It was becoming annoyingly familiar. Somehow when he was around, she never managed to bowl him over with anything but amusement—at her expense.

There was one notable exception. He'd admired her expertise with horses. She remembered the way his compliment had made her glow. And she wanted more. She wanted him to notice her as a woman. If she could impress a sophisticated man like Dawson Prescott, surely she wouldn't have any trouble attracting the cowboy she knew would be her soul mate.

''Since I wasn't there, it's hard to know why no one approached you,'' Willa said. She pushed her glasses up more securely on her nose. ''You're a bright, talented woman. If they were too nearsighted to notice, it's their loss.''

''Thanks for trying, Willa, but I'm not buying it.'' Mattie leveled a look at Jillian. ''You were there. If I'm not a two-bagger, maybe it was because of Brody.''

The other woman shook her head. ''I kept him on the dance floor and away from you as much as possible. I'm carrying around a lot of extra weight these days and still managed to dance his tootsies off until he begged for mercy. Poor guy. It was awful.''

Willa laughed. ''By the look on your face, I can tell it was a great hardship and sheer torture.''

Jillian dramatically rested the back of her hand on her forehead. ''It was just dreadful, hideous, and—'' She started laughing. ''Who am I kidding? I can't wait to be Mrs. Brody Fortune.''

Mattie sighed. ''If it wasn't because of him, then maybe it was because of Dawson. Do you think the men in the place thought we were together? A couple? And that's why no one hit on me?''

Jillian thought a minute, then shook her head. ''Not a chance. You had your arms folded over your chest. Very closed body language. And he looked like he was on high alert, guarding the world's only chocolate stash. Not to mention the fact that you hardly talked to each other, let alone exchanged longing looks. Then again, you kept dashing to the ladies' room every two minutes.'' She shook her head. ''I don't think anyone, even the relationship-challenged, would have mistaken you two for a couple.''

''Then what *is* it? What's wrong with me?'' Mattie put her fork down and crossed her arms over her chest, looking from one woman to the other.

''There's nothing wrong with you, Mattie,'' Jillian said. Then she glanced at Willa, who gave her what looked like a go-ahead nod. ''Nothing that a little makeover wouldn't cure.''

''Makeover? What do you mean?'' Mattie asked.

Willa sipped her iced tea, then said, ''She means a haircut and cosmetics lesson.''

''What good will that do?'' Mattie asked, disappointed.

"Did you ever see the movie *My Fair Lady?*" Willa asked, leaning forward.

"Yes," Mattie answered.

"Jillian and I are going to play Professor Higgins and Colonel Pickering."

"Eliza Doolittle spent a lot of time working on the way she talked," Mattie said. "If you're telling me I need to lose the accent—"

"Not on your life," Willa said. "It's adorable. A great gimmick to meet men. You just need some pizzazz. Some style to your hair and makeup to show off your assets."

"She's right, Mattie. Your features are wonderful. And women pay a lot of money to dye their hair the same color as yours. You have all the raw material to be a femme fatale. But you don't know what to do with it. Hasn't anyone ever shown you how to apply makeup?"

"My mother tried everything she could think of to clean me up. She said I would never find a husband if I didn't put on a dress once in a while." Mattie shrugged. "I was too stubborn. As much as I hate to admit it, mother may have been right."

Jillian shook her head. "I'm not sure the dress is necessary. With some sexy shaping to your hair, a little eye shadow and mascara, I don't think men will care what you're wearing. In fact, Willa and I would be wise to stand clear. In my condition it wouldn't be smart to get in the way of the male stampede."

Mattie glanced uncertainly at each of them. "I suppose it's worth a try. But I don't know where to go. What do I have to do?"

Jillian smiled and stood up, then signaled the waitress for their check. "There's a place right around the corner, just down the street from the corporate office. I found it after work one day. The hairstylist is wonderful, and they also have an esthetician.''

Mattie frowned. ''A what?''

''It's a fancy name for someone who goes to school to learn about skin care and cosmetics. Carol Donnelly is wonderful. She's going to do my makeup for the wedding. Let's drop in and see if they can squeeze you in. What do you say?''

Mattie wasn't sure whether to be excited or afraid— very afraid. But she wasn't happy with herself the way she was. If these two women whom she liked and admired thought she should change her look, then she was in. After all, what did she have to lose? If anyone laughed, she could wear a hat until her hair grew back.

Willa stood up. ''C'mon, Mattie. Aren't you finished eating yet? We have people to see, hair to cut, greasepaint to apply. And we have to do it before you chicken out.''

''Matilda Fortune, don't be a wimp. Open your eyes,'' Willa said.

''How does my hair look? Willa? Jillian? Are you afraid to tell me? Now I really do need a bag over my head. Right?''

''No guts, no glory,'' Jillian said, laughter in her voice.

Mattie opened one eye. First impression: sleek, shiny hair. Okay. She slowly opened her other eye.

''What do you think?'' the stylist asked expectantly.

Wisps of golden highlighted hair fell softly over her forehead. Layers gently framed her face and the curled-under neckline barely brushed the collar of her cotton shirt. She shook her head slightly, feeling the silky hair move. What a lovely sensation. The best part was that she *looked* pretty darn good. At least, *she* thought so. But then, she was beginning to wonder if she had any judgment.

"Well?" Jillian asked, hands on her hips. "Aren't you going to say something?"

Mattie grinned. "I guess I don't have to wear a bag over my head."

"Now there's high praise," Willa said dryly. "You look fabulous."

"I think I like it." She looked at the stylist. "But I'm sure I won't be able to make it look like this."

"You have natural wave, so all you need is a blow-dryer to give it some fullness. The cut should hold up great even if you let it air-dry straight from the shower. Just bend over, shake your head, and it will fall into place. Perfect for an outdoorsy woman like yourself."

"One down, one to go," Jillian said. "I think Carol's ready for you."

Mattie shook her head. Partly a negative response, partly because her hair felt so wonderful, loose and free. But the best part was that it did fall right back into place.

"Carol will never be ready for me," she said skeptically. She couldn't be so lucky as to have the woman turn plain-Jane Matilda Fortune into a woman that a man would look at twice.

"Wanna bet?" Jillian asked. "This time you have to keep your eyes open. She'll teach you how to do everything."

A few minutes later, Jillian and Willa waited in a nearby lounge while Mattie sat in front of a mirror surrounded by theatrical lights. Carol, a beautiful sophisticated blonde, was checking over Mattie's filled-out questionnaire. Then she pulled out creams, brushes and containers of cosmetics and went to work.

For the next hour, Mattie concentrated on everything the esthetician said. She learned about moisturizer and foundation and how to apply them for a flawless look. Learned about cosmetics and daytime versus nighttime looks.

When Carol was finished, Mattie stared at herself in the mirror. "I can't believe it's me," she said reverently. She was beginning to believe in miracles.

"You look sensational. If I do say so myself," Carol said, and stepped back.

Mattie continued to study her reflection. "If I hadn't seen it with my own eyes," she breathed, "I wouldn't have believed it possible."

Carol smiled, genuinely pleased. "Let's go show your friends."

Impulsively, Mattie jumped out of the chair and hugged the other woman. "You're a miracle worker."

The woman shook her head. "You're a beautiful woman. I just brought it out."

Mattie walked down the hall and found Jillian and Willa in the lounge, reading magazines. When she entered the room, the two women stared openmouthed and speechless for several moments. That was a miracle in itself.

Jillian blinked. "You're an absolute stunner, Mattie Fortune. I can't believe it."

"That goes double for me," Willa said. "I knew a makeover would help, but I didn't know a supermodel would be born."

"You're exaggerating," Mattie said, finding it difficult to believe, even though she so desperately wanted to.

"Only a little."

Mattie nodded. And she couldn't wait until Dawson Prescott got a look at her. She wanted to bowl him over. Only a little.

Because if she passed *his* test, she planned to go on—to find her soul mate.

Dawson had always loved spending time at the Double Crown, and today was no exception. He just wished that keeping tabs on Mattie wasn't what had brought him here. He'd used the excuse of needing to take a ride on horseback to clear his head and relax on a beautiful Saturday afternoon.

In truth, he was here to check up on Mattie, to see with his own eyes that she was okay. He'd called the previous day and been told that she was bridal shopping with Jillian and Willa. He'd congratulated himself on being off the hook for a while. How much trouble could she get into with a college professor and a pregnant bride-to-be?

But today he'd felt restless. It had been over twenty-four hours since he'd actually seen the sassy Aussie. He wished it had been that long since he'd thought about her. She had an annoying way of creeping into his mind at the weirdest times: in business meetings, in his dreams, first thing in the morning. But as he walked to the barn to find her, he reminded himself that he was just doing his duty. He would make certain that she was all right.

He needed to see that she was present and accounted for and hadn't run off with one of the cowboys. He smiled at the thought. Since Griff had left, she'd been on the prowl with little success. His grin widened as he remembered poker night. Bobby Lee and Ethan had welcomed her with less than open-armed enthusiasm. Then when she'd started winning, they couldn't get rid of her fast enough.

And at the Watering Hole, she had been as obvious as all get out, walking to the ladies' room every two minutes. He'd caught a couple of guys giving her legs the once-over. But with one look Dawson conveyed his message: Look but don't touch if you know what's good for you.

He figured he had this covert assignment wired. Griff had called to say he would be home a few days before the wedding. When he knew an exact date, he said, he would let Dawson know. But Mattie had struck out twice with men. Dawson decided the odds were in his favor that her inning would end without a score, so he had nothing to worry about on his watch. He would play the part of surrogate big brother a little while longer to the little girl from Australia.

As he drew closer to the barn, he noticed a group of cowboys standing by the corral. He wondered if there was a problem, but when laughter drifted to him, he decided not. As the bodies shifted, he noticed a woman at the center of the gathering and wondered who she was. Loose blond hair tickled her collar, but he couldn't think of any female on the ranch who wore her hair that way. His gaze lowered to her trim waist, where her shirt was tucked into worn jeans that hugged her curvy hips. Whoever she was, her figure should be registered as a lethal weapon. Then he looked lower and noticed her long, shapely legs. He'd had dreams—day and night—about those legs.

Mattie? Surrounded by men?

Increasing his pace, he arrived just in time to hear one of the cowboys say, "C'mon down to the bunkhouse later, Mattie. Ethan's plannin' to teach us a new card game.''

''I'll be there,'' she said. ''Thanks for asking.'' Her voice drifted to him. When had it turned so sweet and musical that she could play his insides like a violin?

''Hey, look who's here. How's it going, Dawson?'' Bobby Lee stuck his hand out.

Dawson took it as he glared at the four ranch hands gathered around Mattie. ''What's going on?'' he asked.

Bobby Lee frowned. ''Not much. How about you? Something wrong? You look like someone kicked your dog and stole your favorite horse, partner.''

Mattie turned to look at him. If it hadn't been for the legs that had haunted him, he probably wouldn't have recognized her. Her hair! It hung silky, sexy and loose around her face in a very flattering style. Her eyes looked bigger and grayer than he'd ever noticed before. And she was wearing lipstick! He felt like he'd been jabbed in the gut with a two-by-four, knocking the air from his lungs.

Mattie Fortune was beautiful.

When he could take his eyes off her, he got a better look at all the cowboys who were drooling over her.

''Hi, Dawson. What are you doing here?'' she asked, watching him carefully.

Pull it together, he told himself. He would give her the same story he'd used at the house when he'd arrived. ''I needed a ride to clear my head.''

''That's a wonderful idea,'' she said. ''You spend way too much time indoors playing with your numbers.''

He wanted to shoot back a clever rejoinder. But he looked at the stunning woman before him and couldn't form a coherent thought, let alone a witty retort. And in any case, it would be a lie. No matter how much he might want it to be so, she wasn't a child. She was exactly what she'd been saying she was—a full-grown woman.

Bobby Lee shuffled his feet. "Pete, why don't you go on into the barn and saddle up Chloe for Dawson?"

A dark-haired, blue-eyed cowboy shook his head, then slid a glance to Mattie. "I'm on my break, boss. Why don't you get Ricky to do it?"

"Can't." The young man looked about sixteen and wore a hat almost as big as he was. "Sprained my wrist. Remember?"

Bobby Lee looked around. "How about you, Will?"

The lanky cowboy shook his head. "Chloe hates my guts. Kept trying to nip me last time I tried to saddle her."

"She knows you don't like her," Mattie said.

It was as if they were circling the wagons around her. He was the guy in the black hat who planned to carry her off. *Not in this lifetime.* Besides that, Dawson suspected no one wanted to leave and get cut from the herd. This assignment to watch over her had somehow slipped from his control. That was unacceptable. Dawson knew he had to do something to get her away from them.

When he couldn't come up with anything that didn't make him look like a jerk, he decided to go saddle his own horse. He would take his sweet time and hope their breaks were over when he was through. Or that he had a plan to put her ladyship safely under his guard.

"Thanks all the same, fellas. But I can saddle

Chloe. Mattie likes to joke about my job. But the truth is, I've been riding for years on the Double Crown, and Chloe actually likes me.'' He gave the group of them the same look he'd used to keep the prowling cowboys at the Watering Hole away from Mattie. He prayed it would have the same result.

He moved past the group and headed to the barn. Moments later he heard footsteps behind him.

"Dawson? Wait up."

Mattie. He breathed a sigh of relief, then turned. "What?"

"I'm coming with you. Chloe was favoring her back leg the last time you rode her—that day we took the schoolkids riding. I checked her, but want to give it a look."

"Okay." He looked over her head and didn't miss the dark looks sent his way. He wished he could tell the cowboys that when his assignment was done, they were all welcome to try their luck with Mattie—and her brother Griff. But not a day sooner.

They entered the barn, and Dawson allowed his eyes to adjust to the dimness. That only seemed to enhance his other senses. Over the scents of hay and horses, he didn't miss Mattie's fragrance. As she lifted the horse's leg for a look-see, he worked on getting his galloping pulse under control. Talk about being caught between a rock and a hard place. He was the scum of the earth for what he was thinking about her. He wanted her. But although she looked like a grown woman, she was still way too young for him—a big clue that he needed some distance. Yet he couldn't back off and let anyone else move in. Not until Griff was back.

"Would you mind if I rode with you?" Mattie asked, looking up at him.

"Not at all," he answered. His prayer was answered. He could keep her under his watchful eye without making her suspicious of his motives. "Why?"

"I can't find anything wrong with her, but I want to watch her walk."

"Okay. You can come." Odd. He was annoyed that her reason was the horse and not a desire to be with him.

But it was good news that she would be away from the lecherous cowboys and safe with him. The bad news was that she would be with him. Safe? He couldn't swear to it. Not when he had to look into her beautiful face and pretend he couldn't care less.

The best way to handle this was to make her believe he hadn't noticed the change in her. Besides, once he got used to it, surely the feelings would go away.

"Last one in the saddle is a rotten egg," he said.

"You're on."

Her sudden, sunny, stunning smile would have knocked him out of the saddle if he'd already been in one. He was brighter than the average bear, but it didn't take a mental giant to see that this was a really bad idea.

Five

"How nice that you can stay for dinner, Dawson." Aunt Lily smiled at him.

"I appreciate the invitation. Not to mention the effervescent, charming company," he answered.

Mattie realized her own feelings echoed her aunt's words, but her reasons were quite different. She and Dawson had ridden all afternoon, which normally would have put her in a wonderful mood—the riding, the fresh air, the horses. Except for the company.

Dawson Prescott unsettled her too much to produce anything even close to peace of mind. But now they were cleaned up and visiting in the great room. Her aunt sat on the sofa facing the hearth, and she and Dawson occupied chairs across from each other with a coffee table between them. A crackling blaze filled the fireplace.

Mattie felt a little crackly herself, and just a bit hot, maybe enough to spit sparks. She had spent hours with Dawson and he hadn't mentioned a single word about the difference in her appearance. Maybe he thought she looked better the other way. If he did, he was the only one, because everyone else had given her a thumbs-up on the new look. Some of the ranch hands had snapped their heads around so fast for a double take, she wondered if the local chiropractor had an epidemic of whiplash on his hands.

She grinned at the thought, but it faded fast. For some reason she didn't understand, Dawson's vote on her change carried more weight than anyone else's— probably because he'd given her such a hard time about looking like a kid. Since he was hanging around for supper, she might be able to coerce a confession from him that she looked grown-up now.

"I think Dawson has an ulterior motive for staying to dinner, Aunt Lily," Mattie said to her aunt. "Something that has nothing to do with the Fortune charm or effervescence. He told me this afternoon that his house is being redecorated, and he can't stand the chaos."

"Then by all means, you must stay," Lily said to him.

"Thank you, Lily," he said, shooting a look at Mattie that said, loudly and clearly, he wished she would mind her own business.

She just smiled smugly at him.

"You're very welcome, Dawson. In fact, if you need to move in for a while, please feel free. After all, that's why Willa is here. Thank goodness for that, or we wouldn't have the pleasure of her company. And we'd love to have the pleasure of yours." Before Mattie could speak for herself, her aunt continued, "Except tonight it's just Mattie who will have the job of entertaining you."

"What?" Mattie asked.

Her and her big mouth. She had just been having a little fun at Dawson's expense. Now he practically had an engraved invitation to move in. But she figured he wouldn't do it. After all, she was here and her presence would no doubt discourage him. Although, she had to admit, she had seen more of him in the last four days than she had since her arrival in Texas a few months before.

"Why just me?" she asked.

"We're taking Willa to that new restaurant in San Antonio and to the theater. There's a touring company in town. She's upstairs getting ready now. If it were just Ryan and me, we would cancel. But Willa—"

"Don't change your plans on my account," Dawson said. "I've heard that the show is good. Go. Have a wonderful time."

"If you're sure," she said doubtfully.

"I'd feel terrible if you canceled on my account." He leaned forward and rested his forearms on his knees.

"All right, then. And actually, I'm glad you'll be here to keep Mattie company." Lily sent him a grateful look. "I was feeling horribly guilty about leaving her alone."

There was amusement in Dawson's eyes when he looked her way, and Mattie had the urge to duck and run for cover. She knew there was a zinger in her near future.

"I'll make sure Mattie doesn't get into any trouble while you're gone," he said. "I don't mind baby-sitting."

Zinger, as expected. Sometimes Mattie hated when she was right. "I may be young, Dawson, but at least I wasn't raised by wolves. I'm well aware that it's not polite to talk in front of people as if they're not in the room." Mattie glanced apologetically at her aunt. "No offense, Aunt Lily. I didn't mean you."

"None taken, dear."

Dawson leaned back in his chair and rested one ankle across the opposite knee—a supremely confident pose. And very male. "Actually, I'm from the chil-dren-should-be-seen-and-not-heard school of child rearing," he shot back at her.

"You don't say," Mattie answered. *Awesome comeback, Mattie,* she said to herself. *Guess you told him, but good.* Her only excuse for dull wit was the annoying fluttering of her heart. It had started when Dawson assumed that masculine pose in the chair. It continued no matter how he moved, and wouldn't let up. Apparently she was experiencing lack of blood flow to the brain.

Dawson gave her a small—and, she thought, pity-ing—smile, then met her aunt's gaze again. "I'm glad to be of service in the chaperone department. Kids these days," he said shaking his head. "Can't be too careful. She might throw a wild party while the folks are gone."

Mattie considered it a moral victory that she didn't choke him. So much for making him see her as a woman. How could she get him to stop treating her like a child? What was it going to take to get his attention?

Lily laughed. "I'm sure Mattie can take care of her-self. We offered to get her a ticket to the play, but she wasn't interested. But with you here, I won't feel so concerned about leaving her alone. Clint Lockhart is still on the loose after that shocking prison escape, and we can't take any chances."

"No worries, Aunt Lily. Dawson and I will take good care of the place while you're gone." She glared at him again, in case he'd missed the last one. "And no wild parties, I promise."

"Hello, everyone." Uncle Ryan walked into the great room with Willa on his left arm. He wore a charcoal-colored suit with a crisp white shirt and red tie. His goddaughter had on a black dress that seemed to hug her slender body like a second skin. "I found this sweet young thing in the hall upstairs, and she allowed me to escort her down."

"Hello, Dawson. Mattie," Willa said, blushing at Ryan's compliment.

She raised one eyebrow, and Mattie knew what she was asking. Had anyone noticed her new look? Just everyone but Dawson! she wanted to shout. Instead, she angled her head toward him and surreptitiously shook her head at her friend. Willa's mouth thinned as she frowned at him.

Mattie glanced at Dawson to see if he'd noticed, and caught him looking Willa over. Since his gaze went from her neckline to the hem of that *va-va-voom* dress, she figured he'd missed the other woman's disapproval. Her heart fell when she saw the definite gleam in his hazel eyes.

Blockhead, she thought. Apparently he was immune to the many faces of Mattie Fortune. It didn't make much difference whether it was the old outback look or the new and improved Texas temptress. He couldn't care less. The depth of her disappointment surprised her. Did she really give a darn what he thought of her?

Lily walked over to her husband and kissed his lean cheek. "You look wonderful, dear," she said.

"Not as wonderful as you, darling. You take my breath away." He took in her appearance, the red dress that showed a subtle amount of cleavage yet still managed to look sexy. "I will be the envy of every man who sees us tonight, escorting these two beautiful women."

"I envy you," Dawson said fervently.

Ryan met Mattie's gaze. "If you were going, I would need a whip and a chair to protect you from all the men, Mattie. I can't believe the difference in you."

Her cheeks grew warm. "Thank you, Uncle Ryan. You're very kind."

"No, I'm not that nice. Just honest. If I had more time, I would continue to sing your praises." He looked at his wife. "But time's a wastin'. Your carriage awaits, my lovely," he said, smiling at her.

"I'll tell you all about it, Mattie," Willa promised.

"Make yourselves at home, you two," Lily said. Ryan held out his arm, and her aunt slipped her hand into the bend of his elbow. A true gentleman, he escorted both women from the room.

Mattie sighed. Just like a fairy tale, she thought. Some day her soul mate would hold out his arm to her. He'd be a man who would notice and appreciate the trouble she went through to look nice for him. A man who didn't have his head buried in mathematical formulas and spreadsheets. A man who would be aware of the people around him and the changes they made.

When they were alone, she said to Dawson, "I'm starved. Are you ready to eat?"

"Yup. Lead the way."

She did, and found Rosita Perez in the kitchen, fussing over a salad and corn bread she'd made to go with the pot of chili bubbling on the stove.

Mattie stood behind her and sniffed. "That smells wonderful, Rosita. You must give me the recipe."

"You, niña? You can cook?" The Mexican woman smiled fondly at her, taking any real or implied sting from her words.

"Could if I had to," she said, aware that it was a

childish comeback. Dawson already thought she was just a kid; she might as well give him reason.

She broke off a corner of the bread and closed her eyes at the heavenly taste and the way it melted in her mouth. ''If I live to be a hundred, I don't think I could ever learn to make anything this good.''

''I was just—how do you say?—busting your chops,'' Rosita said, patting her arm. ''You can cook. If you find a man that you care enough about to please, you would take the time.'' She glanced coyly at Dawson.

Mattie wouldn't hurt the woman's feelings by telling her it would be a cold day in hell before she would search for the way to Dawson's heart. In fact, she had some serious doubts about whether or not he had one. In any case, she refused to look at him. No doubt Rosita's remark had generated that infuriatingly amused expression on his face.

The housekeeper wiped her hands on her apron. ''Everything is ready. I'll serve dinner for you two in the dining room now.''

''Since it is just the two of us, we can eat in the kitchen. Right, Dawson?'' Mattie glanced at him then.

''Fine,'' he said.

He stood a couple of paces behind her with his fingertips tucked into the pockets of his jeans. The long sleeves of his white shirt were rolled to just below the elbow. When her gaze lifted higher, she noticed several dark chest hairs peeking past the button closest to his neck. He looked so sexy, her heart was kicked into a trot. She wished she could get him to notice her in the same way. Just once. But she had a better chance of flapping her arms and flying to the moon.

''Kitchen it is,'' she said, looking down at Rosita.

"And I think you should go home to your husband. Take him some of this wonderful dinner. Although I'm sure you won his heart a long time ago, it can't hurt to remind him. You'll have him wrapped around your pinkie as quick as you can say 'chili con carne.'"

"I don't know," Rosita answered, looking doubtful.

"Mattie's right," Dawson said. "We can clean this up. Enjoy your evening with your husband."

"Sí, señor. If you're sure."

"Absolutely positive," he said. "After all, I'm a guest. Mattie's going to do all the dishes."

Mattie shook her head, disgusted at herself. She was slipping; she hadn't seen that zinger coming. But he wouldn't get away with it. "The night is young. Anything can happen," she said mysteriously.

Rosita chuckled as she hung her apron on the hook in the pantry and grabbed her sweater and purse. "Señorita Matilda, you go, girl."

"No worries," she answered, chuckling at the older woman's comment. "I'll keep him honest."

If she hadn't been looking directly at him, Mattie never would have seen the odd expression that crossed Dawson's face at her casual remark. Was he being less than honest about something? Could it be his nonchalance about her new look? Maybe he really had noticed and was pretending not to. Although, why he would do that was beyond her. But two could play that game.

They said good-night to the housekeeper and watched through the kitchen window as she got into her car. Then Mattie realized they were completely alone in the house. No horses to ride. No cowboys to talk to. No numbers to crunch. Just Dawson and her. Let him try to ignore her now.

It was pride, pure and simple. She tried not to remember her uncle's remark about pride before a fall. Because, by gum, she would get his attention or die trying. Even the cowboys on the ranch had finally taken notice of her new haircut and makeup. They even invited her back to the poker game. That was a step in the right direction to finding her soul mate. Now if she could only figure out why it was such a badge of honor to get Dawson to recognize her as a woman.

They were in the kitchen. She could turn the heat up a degree or two. And she knew just how to go about it. She'd put on her best brown corduroy bib overalls and the cap-sleeved T-shirt that Jillian had said showed off her toned arms. Mattie decided to undo one strap. She'd seen the look in a magazine, and had the urge to see what Mr. Stuffed Shirt would do.

In Dawson's case, the term *stuffed shirt* was apt. Because his shirt was stuffed with some pretty nice muscles. When he wasn't wearing one of those expensive suits, she could almost picture him herding cattle or working with the horses. The things that thought did to her heart rate could revolutionize cardiac care, she decided.

While Dawson started setting the table, Mattie casually unhooked one side of her overalls and let the strap and attached metal hook hang down. Half of the bib folded over, revealing the curve of her breast encased in T-shirt. Before she could see his reaction, the front doorbell rang.

"I'll get it," he said.

When he came back, there was a strange, almost angry look on his face.

"Who was it?" she asked.

"Ethan."

"Really?" she said, pleased that the cowboy had come to the door. She waited for Dawson to give her the message, but he didn't say anything. "Did he have a purpose for ringing the doorbell, or was it just a case of ding-dong ditch?"

"Ding-dong what?"

"Ditch. You know. Kids do it all the time. You ring someone's doorbell, then run away."

He shook his head. "I don't think I ever played that."

She sighed. "Were you ever a child, Dawson?" She held up her hand. "Never mind. Don't answer that. You'll no doubt turn the words back on me, and I'll be sorry I asked." She realized he hadn't told her what Ethan wanted. "What did he say?"

"Who?"

She put her hands on her hips. "Ethan, of course."

"Oh." He stuck the tips of his fingers in his pockets, and took so long to answer that she wasn't sure he was going to come clean. "He said to tell you not to forget the poker game tonight."

"No worries about that," she said, pleased that the cowboy would go out of his way to remind her. "He told me earlier today that the hands usually go to town on Saturday night, but decided to have a game instead. And they thought to ask me. As if I could forget that." When Dawson mumbled something, she asked, "What did you say?"

"Just that I wish you would—" he stopped, searching for words "—put dinner on the table."

"I will when you finish setting it," she answered. "But let me give you a hand."

When she applauded, he sighed and shook his head. Then he lifted plates and bowls out of the cupboard. After setting the salad, a basket of corn bread, and the steaming pot of chili on the table, she sat down.

Dawson was about to do the same when the phone rang. "I'll get it. Stay," he commanded.

Mattie felt like the faithful family pet. *Stay?* She didn't even train horses with commands like that. Semi-annoyed—her usual mental state around Dawson—she watched him. He lifted the receiver, said hello, then asked to take a message. He hung up and joined her at the table, sitting at a right angle to her.

She spooned chili into his bowl and set it on his plate. "Who was that?" she asked.

"Bobby Lee."

He had that tone again, she noticed. The same one he'd used when Ethan had shown up at the front door: a cross between incredulity and irritation. Something told her they were about to play twenty questions again.

"What did he want?" she asked.

"You," he answered.

"I'm sitting—rather *staying* right here. I would have taken it. Why didn't you tell me?"

"Because you're eating dinner."

"Technically, not yet. But I'll ignore that. Did he say *why* he wanted me?"

Dawson had a funny, dark, almost angry look on his face. "Not really. Something about watching a video. If you want, call him back when you finish dinner."

"I'll just call him back now." She started to get up. "Did he leave the number at the bunkhouse?"

One corner of his mouth lifted as he looked far too pleased with himself. "Don't you have it?"

"No, I don't," she said, irritated. "Guess I'll just stop by and see him in case he's not going to the poker game." When he mumbled something again, she asked, "Did you just say 'over my dead body'?"

He shook his head. "I said *bread*. How do you think chili would taste over corn bread?"

"Dreadful," she answered. "And I think you ought to have your *head* examined for even thinking of it."

They started to eat, and she studied him, sliding him looks from beneath her lashes. He was scowling at the food and almost attacked it with his fork. What was wrong with him?

They hadn't taken more than a couple of bites when the doorbell rang again. This time Mattie jumped up before he could. "I'll get it."

"No, let me—" He started to rise.

"Sorry, beat you to it." She hurried through the house and opened the heavy wooden front door. The light beside it was on, illuminating the porch and the walkway beyond. But no one was there. She peered into the darkness, but couldn't see anyone.

Glancing down, Mattie saw a single red rose, and bent to pick it up. She stepped back inside and nearly bumped into Dawson.

"Who was it?" His voice was two parts annoyed, one part angry.

"No one."

"Ding-dong ditch?" he asked, half smiling.

"Not exactly. Someone left this," she answered, holding out the flower for his inspection. "I guess it must be for Willa."

He pointed to the front porch. "There's a note."

Before Mattie could make a move, he bent over to grab it up. Then he shut the door behind him and made a great show of reading the words on the paper. When he finished, all he said was "Hmm."

"Let me see." She reached for it.

He was too quick for her. "Not so fast."

She pointed an accusing finger at him. "You're lying."

"I didn't lie. You have to make a statement to do that. All I said was 'Hmm' and 'Not so fast.'" He raised one eyebrow.

"It's a lie of omission if you let me believe it's for Willa." She tried to get the note again, and he put his hand behind his back. "It's for me, isn't it."

"You're awfully nosy. Not to mention egotistical. Why would you think this is for you?"

"Because I got my hair cut and put on makeup!" She jammed her hands on her hips and glared at him. "You didn't notice?"

"Ah. Is that what's different?" he asked. "I thought there was something."

"Yes, there's something." She heard the angry pitch in her voice and couldn't seem to stop. All the patience and discipline she'd learned to use in dealing with horses went out the window when she was around this exasperating man. And no wonder. He was about as dense and observant as a mule.

He didn't say a word, just continued to stare at her with that amused expression on his face, as if he'd just become aware of the change in her.

She glared at him. "Everyone has noticed. *And* complimented me. Everyone but you. Like I said before, you need to have your eyes examined."

"Actually, if memory serves, you said I should have my head examined."

"So I did. Let me rephrase. Eyesight is the first thing to go as old age creeps up on you. You should have yours checked."

Satisfaction trickled through her at his frown. "Maybe I will," he said.

"Quit stalling, Dawson, and give me the note." She held out her hand.

"Come and get it," he said, waving it under her nose.

"*Now* who's acting like a child?" she asked.

But adrenaline and exhilaration flooded Mattie at his challenge. She felt so alive with the blood singing through her veins. Without warning, she lunged forward and tried to grab the paper, but he snatched it away. He put it behind his back again. She reached around him, got hold of his wrist and tried to pull his arm out—a failing proposition, since he was much more powerful than she.

All's fair in love and war, she thought. Fighting dirty would level the playing field. She reached out and tickled him.

He hunched forward to protect himself, allowing her to pull his arm to her chest. She held it there with one hand, while she tried to pry the paper from his grip with the other. One by one she pulled his fingers away from the note, but he was toying with her. When she just about had what she was after, he closed his hand into a fist again.

She tried to tickle him, but he grabbed her wrists and backed her up against the wall. Using the lower half of his body, he pinned her and rested both of his hands, with hers prisoner in his palms, on the wall on either side of her head. Her breathing was ragged from the exertion. So was his, she noticed. A couple of other things didn't escape her. His eyes held a dark, intense, almost hungry look as his gaze rested on her mouth. And his mouth was barely an inch from hers.

His right eyebrow lifted when he noticed that half of her overalls bib was hanging. The soft material of her T-shirt left little to the imagination, and her bosom, at least half of it, was right there. As he gazed at her, his eyes filled with a tension that she didn't understand, but something about his expression sent a thrill through her. The sensation touched her femininity.

Mattie decided every girl had to experience a first kiss. The brothers Fortune had joined ranks and kept her isolated from the opposite sex. She was five years past sweet sixteen and never been kissed. It was about damn time she knew what it felt like.

By virtue of his gender, Dawson qualified. Since there was nothing between them and never would be, if she did it all wrong, there was nothing to lose. And she would gain practice. She needed that to be able to kiss her soul mate with finesse when she found him. And Dawson was about the best-looking man she'd ever seen. So without further thinking about what she was about to do, she puckered up, leaned forward an inch and pressed her mouth to his.

His lips were soft and warm, rather pleasant, she thought. And very surprised. When he lifted his mouth from hers, a sad little sigh escaped her. He studied her for several long moments. Mattie wasn't sure what he saw in her eyes—maybe her regret that he had ended such a pleasant experience.

A moment later he mumbled, "Oh, hell."

Then he kissed her again, and there was nothing

sweet about it. He slanted his mouth across hers and took charge. Her heart hammered; blood pounded through her veins, a thunderous roar in her ears. She couldn't catch her breath and couldn't find the will to care. Never in her life had she felt anything so exciting, so hot, so wild.

He released her wrists to slide his arms behind her and pull her closer. She savored the freedom to twine her arms around his neck and lean into him. Sensations washed over her, but she didn't miss the hard ridge of his desire pressing against his jeans. A thrill went through her just before Dawson invaded her mouth with his tongue. Instantly her lower body began to throb, creating an aching need. A moan escaped her—

Dawson froze, then pulled his mouth from hers and backed away, still breathing as if he'd run a marathon. Every feminine instinct she possessed cried out in protest. What had she done wrong? He'd kissed her back. She was naive, not stupid. She knew he'd kissed her back. It was wonderful. Surely he'd felt it, too. Had she done something wrong? She couldn't imagine what, but even *she* knew a guy didn't walk away from a hot kiss like that unless there was a problem. Should she know what it was?

She gulped in air and managed to slow her breathing to something close to normal. Mattie wanted desperately to find out why he'd pulled away. But if she asked, he would know that she was a beginner. She felt too vulnerable, too raw, too exposed. The one and only time she had put her heart on the line, she'd been ridiculed.

She couldn't stand it if Dawson made fun of her. He was so convinced she was just a kid. No way would she ask him for pointers to improve her kissing

technique. But she couldn't think of anything to say
as they stood there and stared at each other, both
breathing hard. At least she had the satisfaction of
watching him struggle to draw in air, too. That was a
good thing. Right?

"So," she said, and released a long breath. "Say
something." With great effort she controlled her
voice, trying to keep it light. She thought she suc-
ceeded.

He ran a hand through his hair. "I think I'm going
to take your aunt up on her offer to stay here at the
ranch while my house is being renovated."

Six

Through a haze of out-of-control desire, Dawson studied Mattie's glazed expression, and knew the exact moment his words sank in. She blinked twice, and her gray eyes suddenly caught fire.

A pleased smile pulled at her lips, swollen from his kiss. "It was that good? You're going to hang around for more?" she asked.

He could see she was trying to act savvy and sassy, but he sensed the insecurity lurking at the edges of that grin.

More than anything he could think of at the moment, he wanted another kiss. That was exactly the reason he had to discourage her. His job was to watch over her. The cowboys on the Double Crown were showing far too much interest in her. He figured the best way to do his job was to move to the ranch.

It was his bad luck that he'd figured that out right after kissing Mattie and discovering how very much he enjoyed the experience. On a sliding scale with ten being best, Mattie Fortune was about a fifteen.

His temptation quotient had just multiplied by a hundred, and he would have to spend even more time with her fighting his baser instincts. But with Griff out of town, Brody getting ready for the wedding and Reed on his honeymoon, there was no one he could dump her on. At least, no one he could trust. The question was, just how was he going to explain his decision without A—encouraging another kiss, and B—crushing her spirit when he discouraged her from more kissing.

He took in a deep breath. "It just occurred to me that staying here while my place is being painted would be so much easier."

"Just now you were thinking all that?" she asked. "You mean while we were—you know?"

"Kissing," he answered. "Yeah. I was thinking how much I like the color of these walls. That reminded me of Lily's invitation to stay here. I think I'll take her up on it."

Mattie started pacing. "You mean to tell me you could kiss me like—" she thought for a minute "—like Burt Lancaster kissed Deborah Kerr on that beach in *From Here to Eternity,* and the whole time you were thinking about paint chips?"

"Yeah." He nodded, more determinedly than warranted. Trying to convince himself as well as her. "You could say that." *But it would be a lie.*

"So you dropped me like a hot rock because you were deciding whether or not you want Navajo white or eggshell parfait on your walls?"

"Sort of," he said. He wished Griff hadn't made him promise not to tell her what was going on. He was almost tempted to break that promise, because he hated letting her believe he was that big a jerk. Not to mention how unfair it was to her, keeping her in the dark this way.

"I guess I'll have to practice some more—work on my technique," she said.

"There's nothing wrong with the way you kiss." It had nearly caused *him* to do something they would both regret. He'd been about to carry her off to bed, and he didn't much care whose. He still wanted to, he thought, folding his arms over his chest. Then he leaned a shoulder against the front door. "It's just that this isn't the time or place. And you and I—" He shrugged, hoping she would draw the same conclusion he had: they were like oil and water.

God, this was a mess. The last thing he would ever do was use a woman and toss her aside. His father had done it to his mother, and Dawson had helped her pick up the pieces. Earlier, Mattie had asked him if he'd ever been a kid. The answer she would never hear was no. After his father left, his mom had become angry and increasingly bitter. As a boy, he'd felt more like her counselor than her son. But it had taught him to keep his own relationships superficial so that he'd never hurt anyone.

The sassy Aussie packed a powerful punch. He'd never met a woman like her, and he couldn't help being intrigued. But he would be a fool to let it go any further.

She needed a different kind of man, one who was good at relationships. He wasn't. So showing an interest, then dropping her like a hot rock, as she'd so eloquently put it, would be cavalier and cruel. He wouldn't use Mattie, knowing they couldn't have a future.

"You and me?" she asked, repeating his words. She lifted one eyebrow questioningly. "Interesting thought. Everyone needs a goal." She turned and started to walk away.

He took two steps and grabbed her arm. "And what goal would that be?" He braced himself for the answer he somehow knew he wasn't going to like.

"To make you forget about paint chips *and* your number crunching." She removed his hand from her arm.

That was two goals, but now wasn't the time to point that out. "Mattie, you need to—"

Ignoring him, she turned on her heel and headed for the kitchen.

"Wait—" Dawson started to follow, and the toe of his boot nudged something. Looking down, he saw the rose she'd dropped on the floor when she'd wrapped her arms around his neck. At least he'd made her forget to ask who'd left the rose. Unless she brought it up, he didn't plan to volunteer it was from Ethan.

Even now, the memory sent the blood rushing through his veins in a southerly direction. He was painfully hard. It had taken every ounce of his self-control not to lift her off the floor and urge her to wrap those long legs of hers around his waist—right in the foyer of her uncle's home. If that wasn't bad enough, her uncle Ryan was his friend and a man he respected more than he had his own father. And Dawson worked at the family company. How could he take advantage of the man's niece like this? Dawson figured there had to be something wrong with him to behave this way. But he couldn't seem to help himself.

More than anything, he needed to turn his back on Mattie Fortune before this crazy attraction got too hot to handle. But judging by the calls, drop-ins and secret admirers, every cowboy on the Double Crown felt the same way about Mattie that he did. And she didn't plan to do anything to discourage the attention.

That really chapped his hide.

He bent down and picked up the flower, then placed

it on the table in the foyer. He needed to stay close to her. Just until Griff got back, he amended.

He shook his head. This was nuts. His life was out of control. It had started with his promise to Griff, and had gotten worse with Mattie's new look.

Haircut plus lipstick equaled trouble.

Mattie had never been so irritated and frustrated in her whole life. It had been two weeks since she and Dawson had kissed. On the heels of that life-altering experience, he had insisted on escorting her to the poker game that same night. It had given her immense satisfaction when the ranch hands were not nearly as glad to see him as they'd been the first time. In fact, they had practically ignored him and fallen all over themselves in their attention to her.

She shook her head and angrily jammed the shovel into the muck on the stall floor. It's what she had longed for since her arrival in Texas. But the timing of all that attention was the pits. If only it had happened before she'd kissed Dawson. What the heck had she been thinking? How could she ever have believed that it would be harmless? A test? Practice?

At least Dawson hadn't laughed at her, like her one and only crush had before they'd ever gotten to the kissing stage. And Dawson hadn't taunted her with her plain-Jane nickname. He'd just been thinking about paint chips. Disgusted, she shook her head.

It had been two weeks and there hadn't been a single opportunity to follow up on her challenge to make him forget about paint.

"Perverse man," she grumbled to herself.

Every time she thought about Dawson, his arms around her, his mouth pressed to hers, she got that warm, tight feeling low in her abdomen. Then a throbbing started between her legs. She'd thought that kissing him would somehow bring her closer to her goal of finding a soul mate and creating a family. But she had discovered that kissing a man once was like trying to eat one piece of chocolate. It couldn't be done. She wanted more. What she'd gotten was a long, disappointing dry spell. And more frustration than any woman should suffer.

Not to mention questions—lots of 'em.

The most important being, would it be as much fun with another man? Oddly enough, she wasn't anxious to do the deed with anyone else. She wanted to try again with Dawson. But since she wasn't getting any younger, she had to hedge her bets. She was ready, willing and able to find a man who would assist in her research to discover if kissing just any man would be as good as it was with Dawson.

There was just one little problem. Actually, he was just under six feet tall and had some serious muscles that made him more of a *big* problem.

Dawson Prescott.

He'd moved into her brother's room at the Double Crown. Just until Griff came back, he'd said. Although there'd been some delays, he was sure the house renovations would be finished just about the same time her brother returned. On top of everything else, the man was a psychic? No one ever knew when Griff would return, let alone tried to coordinate it with redecorating.

She shoveled more stall muck into the waiting wheelbarrow. Ever since Dawson had moved to the ranch, Mattie couldn't turn around without bumping into him. He was there when she fed the horses. He dropped by during her training sessions. He turned up when she was hanging out with the other cowboys. He was always underfoot, because he was crunching his numbers right here on the ranch. He claimed to be getting more accomplished by using the phone and fax that her uncle had set up on the premises than by driving to the office in San Antonio.

There was one thing she was starting to learn about Dawson: things could always get worse. It wasn't so bad that he was sleeping in the room next to hers. But there was a bathroom in between that they shared. She could hear him taking a shower, which he seemed to take great delight in doing every night. In her own room, minding her own business, she was forced to listen to him. And listening forced her imagination into high gear. She couldn't help picturing all his manly muscles naked, wet, soapy and sleek. He was the devil in—or out of—an expensive suit.

For the rest of her life was she doomed, when she heard a shower go on, to get hot all over? Or feel the blood rush through her? Or experience a sensation at her very center that made her feel as if she would explode? Whenever a man's deep voice broke into a rendition—a very bad rendition—of Don't Fence Me In, would she want desperately to kiss him?

"Wait until I tell him he couldn't carry a tune in a duffel bag," she complained to herself.

"Who can't carry a tune?"

Dawson. Without turning around, she closed her eyes and shook her head. She wasn't in any mood to be nice to him. "For a stuffed-shirt city slicker, you sure have a knack for sneaking up on a body."

"Thank you," he said brightly. "Although you

must have been deep in thought. I made enough noise to wake the dead.''

His voice was so cheerful, she wanted to scream. She turned around, and hated the fact that her gaze automatically zeroed in on his mouth. "That wasn't a compliment."

"Oh. Could've fooled me."

"Yeah, there's a lot of that going around," she said, thinking about his kiss. "What are you doing here?"

He folded his arms over his chest and leaned against the metal fence. "I was in the way up at the house."

Here, too, she wanted to say. Her mother would've been proud of the way she held her tongue. "What's going on up there?"

"Wedding preparations. Deliveries. Hustle. Bustle. It's starting."

"'Bout time. The festivities are five days away. People will be arriving. Reed and Mallory are supposed to be back from their honeymoon that morning." She sighed and settled her chin on her gloved hand that rested on the shovel.

"That was a very thoughtful sound," he said. "What brought that on?"

"I was just wondering if Griff will make it home in time for Brody and Jillian's wedding."

"He said he would."

That piqued her curiosity. "When did you talk to him? Seems to me your paths wouldn't have much reason to cross."

His fraction-of-a-second hesitation made her wonder. Then he said in a voice as smooth as a vanilla shake, "The day he left, he stopped by the corporate offices to say goodbye to Brody. Since we were involved in a business meeting, I happened to be there."

Mattie would swear he looked guilty, but she couldn't imagine why. Apparently her imagination only worked when it was accompanied by the sound of a running shower.

"And what did he say about coming home?" she asked.

"He said he didn't know for sure when he would be back. But he would do his best to make it home for the wedding."

She sighed again. "I hope he's all right. I worry about him with all this clandestine stuff."

"I'm sure he's fine," Dawson said. He moved away from the fence and stood in front of her. He lifted her chin with his finger and forced her to meet his gaze. "He's one of the good guys, Mattie. The good guys always win and return to hearth and home. Stiff upper lip, kiddo."

Mattie struggled with her emotional response to his touch and his words. She couldn't breathe a sigh of relief until she saw Griff again and knew for a fact he was safe and sound. With Dawson standing so close to her, her heart went into a state of serious flutter, and she could hardly breathe at all. Then his last words sank in and she realized how Dawson had just addressed her. Kiddo, indeed!

What was it going to take for him to acknowledge the fact that she was a woman?

At the rate he kept turning up, she couldn't help thinking he liked her and wanted to spend time with her. But then, he never did anything but engage in idle chitchat. Like now.

"Dawson, was there some reason you came down here?" she asked testily.

"I told you. I was in the way up at the house."

"Yeah. But this is a really big ranch. There are lots of places you could have gone to be out of the way. What are you doing right *here?*" she asked, pointing to a pile of hay and horse muck. "I might be tempted to think that you actually enjoy my company."

"What in the world would make you think that?" he answered, a half smile pulling at his attractive mouth.

"It doesn't take a doctorate to figure out that like a bad penny, you keep turning up. I can hardly turn around without bumping into you. What's that all about, if you don't want to see me?"

"There could be a couple of reasons."

"Such as?"

"I'm a masochist."

"You don't strike me as the kind of man who has a taste for suffering."

"And how *do* I strike you, exactly?"

She studied him and said seriously, "I can't shake the feeling that you've been hurt by someone."

There was a hollow, self-conscious sound to his laugh. "You know, Mattie, that horse-listening stuff only works on the horses. It's wasted on me."

"Okay." She turned away from him and jammed her shovel into the muck on the floor of the stall.

His footsteps rustled the hay behind her. "What makes you think I've been hurt?"

She shrugged as she half turned to glance at him. "A look in your eyes. The way your whole body tenses when I bring up the subject. Body language speaks louder and more eloquently, and is more revealing sometimes, than words."

"Is that so?" There was his annoying, amused look again.

How she wanted to wipe that expression off his face. She turned away. "Yes, it's so. Although," she added, unable to resist tweaking him the way he did her, "it's interesting the way you tease me about my age, call me 'kiddo,' and pretend that I'm not grown-up."

"And your point would be?"

"You're afraid to see me as a woman." She was shooting in the dark, trying to goad him.

He laughed. "Is that so? Who died and made you the resident shrink?"

"Suit yourself, Dawson. Hide from the truth. But sooner or later, you're going to have to face the fact that I am a woman. Hear me roar."

"When hell freezes over." His tone was angry. Before she could call him on it, he left her alone again.

Where was Mattie?

After dinner, Dawson had excused himself to Lily and Ryan and decided to take a look around the place. Her aunt and uncle hadn't seemed concerned about her absence. They said she frequently got caught up in work and came in late. That first night of checking up on her for Griff, they'd shared dinner because her work had kept her out.

But that was before she had blossomed into someone who looked like a supermodel-in-training, he reminded himself. Before every man on the place had noticed that she was a knockout and started beating a path to her door.

Now he had to step up his surveillance. The downside was that his excuses were getting thin. Starting with his house painting. Which had been completed a week ago. And ending with that very afternoon, when he'd claimed wedding preparations had driven him out of the big house.

He stuck his hands in his pockets and hunched his shoulders against the chilly November evening. It was a beautiful night. Stars glittered in the sky like gold dust on black velvet. He hoped Mattie wasn't enjoying it with a would-be Casanova cowboy. The thought tied him up in knots.

Because of the promise he'd made to her brother. And for no other reason.

He continued the half-mile walk to the barn, alternately hoping that's where he would find her and wondering what he would say to explain his appearance if he did.

Off the top of his head, he could think of two reasons that Griff had better get back soon. One, Dawson knew there was work piling up at the office that he couldn't handle long distance. In fact, there was a mandatory meeting with Brody the following day, and he wasn't sure how he could be in two places at once. Because no way could he leave Mattie alone.

Two, he was running out of excuses for turning up everywhere. Mattie was getting suspicious. What had she called him? Ah, yes. *A bad penny*. Good analogy, he thought. At the very least, he was a bad-penny-in-training.

For the last two weeks he'd been fighting his attraction to her. Every time he saw her, it was more difficult to keep from taking her in his arms and kissing her senseless. It would have been easier if he'd never done it. Then he would just wonder. But he *knew* the soft sweetness of her. The touch, taste and texture of her lips. Her eager, intoxicating response.

And that torturous knowledge was the main reason

for his cold showers every night. Because he knew just one small room separated him from the woman he wanted to touch and taste again. The woman who had set him on fire once, and the one he wanted to go up in flames with.

He got hard just thinking about her. Even the chill Texas night wasn't enough to cool him off.

As he got closer to the barn, he noticed the door was open and there was light coming from inside. When he went inside, the odors of hay, horses and leather assailed him. Then he heard a voice, a man's voice, followed by a female response. Definitely Mattie.

At least they're talking, he thought. But that didn't really make him feel better. A knot of anger squeezed his chest. *That means he's not kissing her.* And for good measure he called out, "Hello."

"Dawson? Is that you?" Mattie called back.

"Yeah."

He followed the voice to the far end of the building closest to the corral. Mattie stood outside Buttercup's stall. One of her legs was bent at the knee as she hooked the heel of her boot in the wooden slat of the gate. It was a blatantly feminine pose that highlighted her slender sexy thigh, and that would have made any man sit up and take notice.

Ethan was no exception. Dawson knew that as surely as he knew one plus one was two. The cowboy stood beside her, his elbow resting on the gate, his fingers a quarter of an inch from her hair, no doubt itching to touch the silky strands. The thumb of his other hand was hooked in his belt, and his fingers angled downward. All his attention was focused on the woman beside him.

If he hadn't kissed her already, Dawson thought, he was fixing to. The idea sent white-hot anger through him.

"What are you doing here so late?" he asked her.

"Ethan stopped by to help me feed the stock. We just got to talking, and time slipped away."

"I see. Hi, Ethan. How's it going?" Dawson asked, he hoped pleasantly.

"Dawson," the other man said, touching the brim of his brown felt hat. "Nice evenin', ain't it?"

"Yeah." It was a lousy evening. He could think of a hundred things he would rather be doing.

"What are you doing here?" Mattie asked him.

He was fresh out of excuses. "Looking for you."

"Really?" She sounded pleased.

He met Ethan's hostile gaze. Dawson knew the younger man was annoyed at the interruption. He looked like a stallion who was staking his claim to a mare and ready to bare his teeth and charge the competition for possession of her. Dawson recognized the expression because it matched his own feelings.

"Would you mind if I talked to Mattie alone?" he asked.

Ethan looked like he minded a lot, but said to Mattie, "That okay with you?"

She nodded. "I'll see you tomorrow."

"Count on it. 'Night," he said to her. "Dawson." His voice couldn't have been colder had it been the iceberg that took out the Titanic.

When they were alone, Mattie turned sideways and rested her elbow on the gate. "So what did you want to see me for?"

"I wondered if you'd like to go into San Antonio with me tomorrow."

"What for?"

"I have a mandatory meeting in the afternoon with your brother to go over the details of the merger between your family's business and your Uncle Ryan's. But afterward, I could take you to the Riverwalk. You haven't been there yet, have you?"

"No."

"I know a great restaurant. The food is good. So is the atmosphere. What do you say?"

"Did you just ask me for a date?" she asked, her eyes teasing, a small smile pulling at the corners of her full mouth.

"I wouldn't call it a date."

She folded her arms over her chest. "Then the answer is no."

"Excuse me?"

She frowned. "When you have your head examined, you might want to have your hearing checked at the same time."

"I heard you just fine," he said.

"So what part of 'no' didn't you understand?"

"The part where you'll go if we call it a date."

"I guess it sounds silly, but since I've been to Texas, I haven't been out on a real, honest-to-goodness date."

And even if she accompanied him tomorrow, she wouldn't be on an honest date. Because he was the slime of the earth, and he was deceiving her. But what choice did he have? He had to be at that meeting. If he left her on the ranch, there was no doubt in his mind that Ethan would move in like a buzzard on a carcass. Dawson was between a rock and a hard place. He just hoped he didn't live to regret this.

He nodded. "Okay, we can call it a date."

She grinned. "Okay, then I'll go."

Seven

"Dawson Prescott, you're the world's biggest blockhead." Jillian glared at him.

"I wasn't thinking," he sheepishly admitted.

"I just can't believe you didn't tell Mattie that Chez Vous is the fanciest restaurant in town and that she would need to wear a dress." Jillian huffed and rolled her eyes in disgust. She gently tapped his temple. "The wheel is spinning but the hamster is out to lunch."

Standing in Brody's lavish outer office at Fortune TX, Ltd., Mattie watched this exchange. Jillian was her brother's assistant as well as his fiancée, and she had decided to work until the day before her wedding, now just four days away.

Watching Jillian needle Dawson, Mattie felt both amusement and despair. She was the "she" they were discussing who didn't have a dress to wear to the fanciest restaurant in town. Dawson had driven them from the ranch in his classy BMW, and they had arrived at the office just minutes before Dawson's mandatory meeting. Jillian had demanded to see the sensational dress Mattie was going to change into for dinner at Chez Vous. Since she had made the reservation at Dawson's request, Jillian knew their destination. But Mattie hadn't brought a dress. She didn't have a dress—shabby *or* sensational.

And Jillian's tirade had begun. Mattie couldn't help feeling a little sorry for Dawson. She did think Jillian was being awfully hard on him.

"I probably should have asked him if I needed to bring anything special with me," Mattie said in his defense.

Jillian shook her head. "No way is he getting off the hook for this, Mattie. Don't you dare be nice to him or feel sorry for him. Brody will be back for the meeting, after he picks up his wedding tux. And you better watch out, Dawson. Why, he'll—"

"What?" Dawson asked, the smile on his face clear evidence that Jillian's outburst didn't bother him a bit. "Challenge me to a duel? Calculators at fifty paces?"

Jillian's glare wasn't nearly as effective when her mouth twitched, indicating she was having a hard time keeping a straight face. "This is nothing to joke about, Dawson."

"I know. And you're right about one thing. I am a blockhead." He met Mattie's gaze. "I'm really sorry. I've had a lot on my mind lately and I just wasn't thinking. It never occurred to me to mention that this place has a pretty fancy dress code."

He really did look like he felt bad for not telling her. Not that it would have mattered, Mattie thought ruefully. Her dress code was jeans. She had nothing fancy.

"No worries," she said shrugging. "We can go somewhere else." Although she couldn't help feeling a little disappointed. The idea of going to a hoity-toity restaurant with a fancy fella like Dawson just once in her life really appealed to her.

"No way are you letting Dawson off the hook," Jillian said emphatically. "The food is fabulous and it's the most expensive place in town. Besides, now Dawson owes you. He needs to pay, big time," she finished, shooting Dawson another phony glare.

"But how can I go?" Mattie asked as she surveyed her best jeans and white cotton shirt. "I don't have anything to wear."

Dawson grinned. "You're probably the only woman I know who can make that statement and be telling the truth."

"Good one, slick. Dig yourself in deeper." Jillian shook her head. "If you ever see a corporate seminar in flattery, I suggest you be first in line to sign up."

He merely grinned back at her. "I'm going to chalk this behavior up to a combination of pregnancy hormones run amok coupled with pre-wedding jitters. Because this is not the politically correct way to treat your boss."

Jillian sniffed. "Technically you're not my boss. Brody is. Although not much longer," she said, leaning back in her chair as she ruefully rubbed her rounded abdomen. "After we're married, I'm joining the ranks of the unemployed until entering the ranks of motherhood. In fact, I'm only still here to keep my sanity before the wedding."

"Yes, and you're doing a fine job of it," Dawson teased.

"I'm sorry to be so hard on you," she apologized. "I forgot that men don't realize how important just the right outfit can be to a woman."

"Yeah," Mattie said. "The right pair of jeans can make the difference between success and failure in training an impressionable young horse."

They all laughed, but inside Mattie was shaking like a bowl of semi-solidified jelly. She had no real clue about dressing properly. Overalls bad, dress good. That was about the extent of her knowledge in this situation. Her mother had tried to get her into more feminine attire. She'd threatened and bribed to no avail. Then she had settled the mother's curse on Mattie: *Put on a dress or you'll never get a husband,* her mother had said.

Mattie glanced at Dawson, so handsome in his three-piece, pin-striped navy-blue suit. Not her first or even second choice for a husband. Although he was good-looking enough to tempt a card-carrying spinster. But she and Dawson were too different. He worked in an office; she was happiest outdoors. His work clothes consisted of suits and ties. Give her a comfortable pair of jeans and scuffed, broken-in boots any day, she thought.

But right now she wasn't worried about the rest of her life. Just a simple dinner.

Mattie rested her hip on the corner of the maple reception desk where Jillian sat. Dawson stood beside her. "I agree with you that he owes me big time. And the restaurant sounds wonderful," she said. "But I still have a problem." They both looked at her. "Where am I going to get a dress on such short notice?"

"I'd offer you something from my closet," Jill said, "but I don't think we're the same size." She shot Dawson a look as she rested her hands on her rounded abdomen. "And no cracks from you about getting my clothes from Omar the tent maker."

"I wouldn't dream of it," he said angelically.

"Mattie is at least two inches taller than I am. So even my pre-pregnancy clothes wouldn't work." Jill thought for a moment, then snapped her fingers and grinned. "I know just the place. It's right around the corner. And you have to go there anyway for the last fitting on your bridesmaid's dress.''

''The bridal boutique?'' Mattie said doubtfully.

The jelly that was her insides started a major bobbling. How would she know what to pick? This was Dawson Prescott—the man she was trying to convince that she was a grown-up. The embarrassment would be too awful if she chose the wrong thing. ''The bridal boutique?'' Mattie said again, her level of doubt just increased tenfold. ''It's just dinner, not the rest of my life.''

''They have lots of after-five dresses. It will be perfect,'' Jill promised. She looked at Dawson. ''And I'm sure my acting boss wouldn't mind a bit if I leave a couple of hours early and help you pick something out. Right, boss?'' She raised one eyebrow suggestively.

''My mama didn't raise a fool,'' he said. ''Anything to keep the pregnant hired help happy.'' He met Mattie's gaze. Pulling out his wallet he said, ''Take my credit card. It will make me feel better.''

''No worries,'' she said, taking it. When Jillian disappeared down the hall and into one of the offices, Mattie looked at Dawson. ''It really is all right if you want to cancel.''

He shook his head. ''This is a date. Remember?''

She certainly did. Sleep had been hard to come by the night before because she'd been so excited. She'd felt like a kid on the night before Christmas. But who knew it would be so complicated?

''We can go somewhere else,'' she said. ''What about the club we all went to that night? The Watering Hole? What I'm wearing would be fine for that.''

His eyes darkened as if he were remembering something unpleasant, then he shook his head emphatically.

"No way. I promised you fancy-schmancy, and that's what you're going to get." He raised one eyebrow, and she knew he was going to zing her. "You're not afraid of buying a dress, are you, Mattie? I promise it won't hurt a bit."

"Is that personal experience talking? Because you've worn so many?" she shot back.

Before he could retort, Jillian returned with her purse slung over her shoulder. "Dawson, you know where Brody's apartment is?" she asked.

He thought for a moment and nodded. "It's the Remington Heights building. On 3rd Avenue."

"That's the place," Jillian said. "I'm fixing dinner for him tonight. When Mattie and I are finished shopping, I'll take her with me so she can get ready. You can pick her up at seven-thirty. Sharp," she said.

He saluted. "Okay, Ma."

Mattie dutifully followed her friend to the elevator. "See you later," she called over her shoulder. She couldn't shake the feeling of being a lamb going to slaughter.

"Shut my mouth and slap me silly." Dawson stared at Mattie. "Who are you and what have you done with that sassy Australian cowgirl?"

He'd thought a haircut and lipstick were trouble. Nothing had prepared him for the one-two punch of the dress she had picked up that afternoon.

"Is it all right?" Standing in Brody's luxurious living room, she nervously glanced down, smoothing an imaginary wrinkle on the black lace covering her thigh.

He broke out in a sweat and swallowed hard.

"You'll do," he said simply, wondering if she noticed his hoarse voice.

Dawson made a circular motion with his finger, indicating she should turn. Although he had a feeling it was tantamount to shooting himself in the foot, he wanted to see her from every angle. He couldn't take his eyes off her. She'd bought a black lace sheath that hugged every one of her delicious curves, starting with just the hint of her breasts visible above the rounded neckline. The proverbial Little Black Dress.

Little was the operative word, he thought, as his gaze lowered. There wasn't enough material in the dress to cover her legs. Just past her thighs, the hem came to an abrupt halt. Not that he was complaining. But he'd thought they were a lethal weapon even encased in denim. Kissed by smoky black nylons, her gams could end the cold war. And in three-inch spike heels, they looked longer, sexier, and more shapely than even his vivid imagination could have produced.

As his gaze swept back up the fascinating length of her, he saw where some of the rest of the dress material was. Around her long, beautiful neck, she wore a choker of matching black lace. And the thought hit him: he wanted to kiss her again—starting with her full lips, lingering a while on that elegant neck, then all the way down to—

"Dawson?" Mattie cleared her throat.

"Hmm?" He shook his head to clear it of the seductive image. Had she been talking to him? "Did you say something?"

"I said I never heard that expression before. 'Shut my mouth and slap me silly.' Does it mean I look all right?" she asked. "Or will they throw me out of Chez Vous on my behind?"

"Oh, yeah," he answered.

"They'll throw me out?" She looked stricken.

He blinked. "No. I mean yes." He let out a long breath. "You look perfect. No one will throw you out of anywhere."

Although he was beginning to wish someone would throw *him* out, preferably on his head to knock some sense into him. If he could rewind the series of events that had put him here, he would have slapped himself sooner and plastered duct tape over his mouth before promising to take her somewhere that required a killer dress. A place that specialized in Texas barbecue would have been just the ticket. Where the hell was his brain? Why had it been so important to take her somewhere for which she needed to dress up like this?

But he knew the answer. He'd figured he needed something spectacular to entice her off the ranch and away from Ethan. Rumor was, she wanted a cowboy. It was Dawson's job to keep her from getting one— at least for a few more days. Therefore, he needed to lure her to his turf. The city.

But the joke was on him. Now he had to spend the evening with her looking like—oh, boy. It suddenly struck him that she'd nailed him when she'd said he was trying to keep her a kid. Somehow he'd known that if he ever acknowledged she was a full-grown woman, he would be in a lot of trouble.

Well, here he was and there she was. No way could he deny that she was all grown-up. A woman. So beautiful he ached with the need to kiss her again, feel the silk of her hair, touch all the soft curves that she'd dressed in black lace for the evening. And no way could he back out of this date. Yup, he was in a lot of trouble. Maybe he could call up reinforcements.

"Where are Brody and Jillian?" he asked. "Maybe they'd like to join us."

"They've already eaten. And she told him she was craving pistachio-nut ice cream, so he took her for some. Besides, they said something about wanting to spend some quiet time alone together because when the wedding festivities start, they won't be able to catch their breath for a while. He said to just lock the door behind us."

No help there, he thought. Taking a deep breath, he decided, damn the torpedoes and full speed ahead. The sooner the better, so he could get this over with. And to some place public enough to take the edge off the temptation she presented.

He held out his arm. "Your chariot awaits, your ladyship."

"Thank you, kind sir," she said, laughing.

The sound went straight through him, leaving a trail of fire in its path. And him in a state of readiness— and need.

Mattie heard the *crunch* of gravel beneath the tires of Dawson's BMW as he guided the luxury car to a stop near the big house on the Double Crown Ranch. He turned off the ignition. The clock on the dash said midnight, the witching hour. And a full moon bathed everything in a silver glow.

Taking a deep breath, he said, "What's the name of that perfume you're wearing? At the restaurant and all the way home I've been trying to think what it's called."

"Something Jillian loaned me. I think it's Seduction. Do you like it?" she asked. She thought she heard him groan.

"It's all right," he said.

"It's pretty pungent in a confined space on a long ride. I hope it didn't bother you."

"Nope. Not a bit," he said. But the normal teasing note was missing from his voice, leaving it curt and just this side of hoarse.

He shifted his position, as if he were uncomfortable. And she thought he groaned again. He was probably stiff after the ride back from town, she decided. Earlier that evening, she had agonized over whether or not she was doing the right thing. Using the correct fork. Presenting the proper image for such an elegant restaurant. After a glass of wine, she had relaxed enough to notice that Dawson was treating her differently. He'd never once called her kiddo, or joked about her needing a baby-sitter or being too young. Had she finally gotten his attention?

Who knew that an expensive scrap of black lace could work such a miracle?

But now she wasn't sure whether or not it was correct to thank him. He had treated her like a woman; she didn't want to make a mistake and remind him of her inexperience.

But good manners were always appropriate, her mother had often said.

"I had a wonderful time tonight, Dawson. Thank you for the date."

"You're welcome. I'm glad you enjoyed yourself. But it's getting late. Time to get you inside. I'll see you to your room." It seemed he couldn't open his door and get out fast enough.

But Mattie wasn't ready for the evening to end just yet. Tonight had been magical. And definitely a lesson in power dressing. She should have listened to her mother a long time ago. Even her inexperience with men didn't keep her from seeing that Dawson couldn't take his eyes off her. And the expression on his face took her breath away.

She couldn't remember what the best food in San Antonio tasted like. But she would never forget the look in his eyes when he first saw her dressed up. She'd wished once to see that amused look wiped off his face. And she finally had. Now she wanted to experiment to see if it might work more magic. Could she get him to kiss her again?

When Dawson opened her door, she hesitated a moment, and he held out his hand. She put hers into his palm, then swung her legs out and let him help her up. When he closed the door, she leaned against it.

"Fresh air," she said with a huge sigh. "It feels good. It's so beautiful tonight."

"Yeah. Beautiful." His voice was deep and masculine.

But what raised goose bumps on her arms was the fact that when he said that, he was looking at her. The feeling that filled her was more intoxicating than the wine she'd had with dinner. For the first time in her life, she actually *felt* beautiful. The whole evening was a fairy tale. She was like Cinderella at the ball. And Dawson her Prince Charming?

He was an awfully cute Mr. P. Charming. All evening her senses had been acute. The scent of his cologne started her insides swing-dancing. Where their bodies had brushed, or he'd touched her hand, heat had quickly followed.

And in the car on the drive back to the ranch, he'd rambled on in that deep, sexy voice of his. He'd pointed out sights of interest along the road, and she'd wondered if he was nervous. She was naive, but not dense. This was Texas, for goodness' sake. It was flat! What sights could there be? There wasn't enough variation to make it as interesting as he was trying to convince her it was. But she had responded as if he'd pointed out a new Wonder of the World. In fact, he'd had her total and complete attention, but not because of what he was saying. The seductive sound of his voice had aroused every cell and nerve in her body. She wanted him to touch her, so much so that she ached from the need.

She shivered, and her teeth chattered in the November night air before she could clamp them together.

"Are you cold?" he asked.

"A little. But I don't mind. The air feels so wonderful. I'd like to enjoy it for a few minutes." She looked at him. "But you don't have to stay." When he didn't say anything, Mattie assumed the evening was over. "Thanks again for a wonderful night, Dawson."

To her surprise, he took off his suit coat and stood in front of her. He dragged the coat around her shoulders. She breathed in the intoxicating scent of him— strong, sexy, seductive.

"Thank you," she whispered. Clearing her throat, she said, "The stars are spectacular."

He moved beside her and leaned against the car, too. Their shoulders brushed, sending sparks dancing through her.

He looked up. "It is something."

"Something? You'll turn a girl's head with that kind of sweet talk."

His deep, wonderful laugh warmed her clear through. Then she thought of something. As a girl who'd never had the opportunity to have her head turned, except for one disastrous time, Mattie wondered what Dawson had been like as a young man courting a girl.

"Dawson, will you tell me something?"

"Maybe. Depends. What do you want to know?"

"When you first started to date, what was your modus operandi?"

He looked down at her, and in the moonlight she could read the amusement on his face. She decided she liked that look and shouldn't let it bother her.

"My M.O.?" he asked. "I'm not sure I had one."

"My brothers tell me that all guys are after the same thing. They perfect the optimum line that will help them get it. What was yours?"

"I can't remember."

"Okay. You don't have to tell me."

"I would if I could." He smiled wryly. "I mean, I really can't recall dating—the early years anyway. I do remember guys who took advantage of the fact that most women want to mother a guy."

His emphasis on the word *most* convinced her that he knew at least one woman who wasn't nurturing. "Most women?" she asked.

"My mother wasn't up to the challenge. Thanks to my father."

"What happened?" she asked. It struck her that he was right about that mothering thing. She heard the pain and anger in his voice, and wanted to make it better. Isn't that what mothers were supposed to do?

"My parents divorced when I was ten," he said. "End of story."

"But—"

"You asked about my teenage technique," he interrupted her. "It wasn't very good. But none of the girls knew any better, either."

Mattie felt like one of those teenage girls. But who better to catch her up to where she should be than an experienced man? A very attractive experienced man? A very attractive, very experienced, very sexy Dawson Prescott.

"So, tell me what you can remember about your technique."

He stuck his fingertips in the pockets of his slacks and laughed as he looked up at the star-studded sky. "It wasn't very sophisticated. Pretty transparent as a matter of fact."

"Don't keep me in suspense. What was it?"

"The submarine races."

"Excuse me?"

"After I spent money on a girl—movie, dinner, that sort of thing—I would take her to what I called my 'thinking place.'"

She rolled her eyes. "Your 'thinking place'?"

"I told you it wasn't very good," he said sheepishly.

"You're right. But this is fascinating. So where was this thinking place, and what does it have to do with submarine races?"

"It was anywhere. Anywhere we could be alone to neck."

"Ah," she said. "Where do the submarine races come in?"

"There was this hill near where I lived that looked out over a valley. My buddies and I would take our dates there and park. To watch the submarine races."

"The girls must have been pretty dense to fall for that line."

"No. I usually picked the eggheads."

"Why?"

"Because they had lots of questions. Curiosity is a teenage boy's best friend."

"You are a sneaky devil."

He laughed and shook his head. "Nope. Just a guy. With my share of testosterone."

"So what happens to the testosterone when you get older?" she asked.

"Why do you ask?" he said sharply.

She shrugged. "Just curious. We've been standing out here for several minutes. Just you and me."

Mattie knew she was flirting with danger. She also knew the way a woman knows these things, that Dawson was attracted to her.

Her feelings about him were confusing, at best. If anyone had asked her a couple of days ago, she would have said she wasn't even sure she liked him. But somehow things had changed tonight. She realized that she liked him very much. She'd waited all evening to be alone with him, really alone. She'd longed for him to kiss her again. She was a grown woman who'd never known the touch of a man. Tonight, she wanted to change that.

"Yup. You and me," he said. "Can't argue with that."

"And you haven't asked me to watch the submarine races yet."

His eyes darkened, confirming her intuition about his attraction. There wasn't a hint of teasing or amusement in his gaze. The look thrilled Mattie to her core and stole the breath from her lungs.

"Do you want to go there, Mattie?"

"More than you can possibly imagine."

Eight

After spending the past few hours with the most beautiful, sexy woman he'd ever met, Dawson had little willpower left—and Mattie was testing it.

All the way back to the ranch he'd smelled her aptly named perfume, listened to the husky sound of her voice in the semidarkness, coupled with the seductive silky whisper of her nylon-clad legs brushing together each time she moved. With every breath he took and every sexy sound she made, he had reminded himself that she was too young, too vulnerable, too off-limits. But for God's sake, he was a man. He wasn't made of stone.

She had to know what she was asking. She just didn't know she was asking the wrong guy. It wasn't fair to do this to the guy who was keeping her safe from this very thing. And it was on the tip of his tongue to tell her so.

"Look, Matt, it's late. We should go in—"

In one angry movement, she pushed away from the car. "I know what you're trying to do, Dawson." She removed his jacket from around her shoulders as if it were distasteful.

"What do you mean?" he asked, trying not to notice the way she was breathing hard and what interesting things that did to the part of her breasts he could see.

"You can't pretend I'm a kid anymore."

Right on that one, he thought, opting for silence as the better part of valor.

"You just used the masculine form of my name." She handed him his jacket. "If you can't bear to touch me, just be honest."

Dawson wanted nothing more than to be honest with her. Unfortunately, it wasn't his secret to reveal. Now he had jumped from the frying pan right smack into the fire. Damn, he wished Griff would get back.

"Mattie, it's not what you think—"

"You don't have a clue what I think. But excuse me if I leave before the portion of the evening where you laugh."

She started to walk away, but he gripped her arm. "Why would you think I would do that?" he asked, angry that she had such a low opinion of him.

"I guess it's my destiny to provide amusement to men." She looked at him, and in the moonlight he saw hurt and rejection on her face. "I fell for a guy once," she said. "A major crush when I was sixteen. He worked on my family's ranch. When I managed the nerve to tell him how I felt, he laughed at me. My nickname was Plain Jane, and he didn't miss the opportunity to use it. But the worst was that he told my brothers. I'd just as soon not repeat that experience— if you don't mind."

She turned on her heel and headed for the house. He followed in her wake through the semidark interior. Lights here and there had been left on for them. It was so quiet, he figured everyone was asleep. He wanted to call out to Mattie to stop, but didn't want to wake her aunt and uncle. Finally she reached the door to her room in their isolated wing of the house. Before he could stop her, she'd stepped inside. He heard the lock *click*.

He stood there a moment, feeling like a jerk. He'd just broken every promise he'd ever made to himself. He'd hurt Mattie. Somehow he had to undo the damage he'd done. He went into the room that adjoined hers and walked through their shared bathroom. When he came out the other side, he saw Mattie still in her dress as she slipped out of her panty hose.

"We have to talk," he said.

"Good Lord!" She gasped and whirled to face him. "You've got to stop sneaking up on me."

"I didn't mean to scare you. I just couldn't end the evening like that."

"Okay. Good night. The end. The pity date is officially over." She turned away and walked over to the dresser, dropping her nylons in the top drawer.

He walked up behind her. In the mirror he saw a single tear slip down her cheek. "Mattie, there's something you need to know."

"I already know everything." She shook her head and said, "All you had to do was say so if you didn't want to kiss me."

"It's not that." He stared at the feminine curve of her neck, at the soft skin that he desperately wanted to taste.

He'd used every last ounce of willpower he possessed to hold himself in check with her outside under the stars. In fact, if he had to guess how he would reap his after-death reward, he figured his self-control tonight qualified him for sainthood. But that could change in the blink of an eye, or the meeting of mouths. If he kissed her, he knew without a doubt that all bets would be off.

He wanted her.

She made a sound that was an awful lot like a sniffle, and he felt his insides twist. *Don't do this to me, Mattie,* he silently begged her.

"Once a plain-Jane, always—" Her voice caught.

"Mattie, that's not true. Do you really not know how beautiful you are?" He couldn't stand it that she would think that. "I wish I could have five minutes alone with the jerk who said that to you." He took her by the shoulders and turned her.

When she looked up at him with misery in her big gray eyes, he knew touching her had been the biggest mistake of his life.

And for reasons he didn't understand, he couldn't seem to care.

He cupped her face in his hands and brushed a single tear from her cheek with his thumb. Then he lowered his mouth to hers. Her lips trembled. At the first touch of their mouths, Mattie's breathing hitched up a notch.

He lifted his head a fraction. "Don't cry, sweetheart. Don't you see? I don't want to hurt you."

She stared at him, seeming to study the tension in his jaw, his eyes. "Then don't walk away from me," she said.

"I don't want to walk away. But there's something you need to know—"

She put her fingers over his mouth to silence him. "I already know everything I need to."

Her hands rested on his waist. She slid them up his chest and around his neck, caressing the hair at his nape. His sharp intake of breath made her smile. Whatever he'd wanted her to know was forgotten. They were in a world all their own, where everyone and everything was forgotten.

He took her face in his hands and touched his lips to hers, a brushing as gentle as the flutter of a butterfly's wings. Yet every part of her came alive at that slight contact. Rational thought washed away on a wave of desire powered by years of yearning. She didn't want to think anymore, only to feel. She found herself caught in a vortex of emotion so powerful she couldn't pull out—and didn't want to.

She felt his chest, the rapid rise and fall. His breathing was less steady than her own. Exhilaration poured through her. This is what she'd been waiting for! She wanted to touch and be touched. To give and receive. She couldn't hold back the feelings any more than she could pluck a star from the sky and cradle it in her hand.

He wrapped his arms around her and deepened the kiss. She felt his tongue trace the seam of her lips, urging them apart. When she willingly complied, he entered her mouth, and she reveled in the fact that she was taking part of his body into her own. To signal her acceptance, she touched his tongue with the tip of hers. He groaned as a shudder shook him.

Pulling back, he gulped in air, then said, "You're a witch."

"Is that good or bad?"

"Definitely good," he mumbled. "I want to make love with you," he whispered. "I want you more than I've ever wanted any woman."

"Then what's stopping you?" she asked.

He went still and met her gaze. "Are you sure? Really and truly certain? I don't want you to have any regrets."

She nodded. "I've never been more certain of anything in my life."

The corners of his mouth turned up slightly, then he kissed her and nibbled his way across her cheek to a general area just beneath her ear.

When he touched *that* spot, it was like a charge of electricity sizzled straight through her body right to her most feminine place. Liquid heat poured through her, and the result was as devastating as the mixture of water and electricity. At the same time, she felt her dress slide off her shoulders and down her body, to land in a pool around her feet.

"And you're a magician," she said, laughing nervously. "That dress came with an instruction manual."

"Where there's a will," he mumbled, tracing that spot again. "And there's definitely a will," he added, his voice husky.

In the next instant her bra loosened, and he lifted one strap from her shoulder and pulled it away. She started to lift her arms to cover her breasts.

He caught her wrists in a gentle grip. "Don't. You're beautiful inside and out."

"Okay," she said, dropping her hands. "If you say so."

"I say so because it's the honest truth."

Her eyes filled again, this time with tears of gratitude. If she'd had any doubts before, they completely disappeared with his words. She trusted Dawson. He wouldn't hurt her. She wanted him to be her first. It was absolutely and completely right.

Boldly, she unbuttoned his shirt and slipped it from his broad shoulders. Moonlight streamed through the windows of her room, and she was never more grateful for Mother Nature's light. In the silver glow, the muscles and contours of Dawson's chest took her breath away. He reached for his belt and the closure on his trousers. Mattie held her breath. She had never seen a naked man before; Dawson was her first.

When he pushed pants and briefs past his hips, his arousal sprang free. He was larger than she'd anticipated, hard and ready. Through her slight flash of fear, she registered satisfaction that he wanted her, too.

He pulled her into his arms and backed her toward the bed. He pulled down the spread and blanket, then gently lifted her. He put one knee on the mattress, then, as if she were delicate crystal, he set her in the center of the double bed. The cool sheet felt wonderful against her hot skin.

He stretched out beside her and pulled her into his arms, naked breasts against his chest. He kissed her again, and the touch of his mouth was electric. He slipped his hand down and cupped her right breast in his big palm, rubbing the pad of his thumb over her nipple. The sensation was so delicious, she held her breath to savor it. Then he shifted his body down and took her into his mouth. He suckled and laved the erect nub with his tongue until the pulse rate between her thighs seemed to vibrate to the rhythm he set.

Then he turned his attention to her other breast and took her to a higher level of wanting. She sank her fingers into his biceps and shuddered with pleasure.

Dawson slid his hand to her waist, cupping it gently before moving downward. He skimmed her abdomen, then his hand slid into the curls between her thighs. With one finger, he traced her opening. Heat radiated from her, and the throbbing at her core became more insistent. Her last conscious thought was that all her fantasies about making love paled in comparison to reality.

He touched the sensitive top of her femininity. "Oh, Dawson—"

"What, sweetheart? Do you want me to stop? If you do," he said, his voice raspy, his chest heaving, "speak now or forever hold your peace. I'm gettin' awfully close to the point of no return—"

"No," she gasped. "Don't you dare stop."

It felt too wonderful for words. When he slid his finger inside her, the pulsating increased. She needed to know the final mystery of mating. She wanted him inside her.

She slid her hand down to his waist, and a groan escaped him. His response nurtured her female soul, and she reveled in her power to turn him on. She started to move her hand lower, then stopped, suddenly shy. He took her fingers and rested them over him. The soft thickness felt right in her hand, like velvet over steel. She stroked him until he groaned.

Suddenly and in one fluid motion, he rolled her to her back, then levered himself on top of her. Spreading her legs wider with his knee, he positioned himself against her. She felt a hard probing at the intimate entrance to her body. She gasped, feeling anticipation as well as a little trepidation. Then he gently pushed.

She felt his passion, his desire, his confusion as he encountered her tightness.

"Mattie, what—" He went still. "Are you—"

Every cell, nerve and muscle in her body screamed out in protest. She had waited for this too long. She was more than ready. He was half a heartbeat from pulling away. No way was he backing out now.

Mattie raised her hips to meet his thrust, and felt

his entry followed by a swift tearing pain. She gasped at the sharp discomfort and buried her face in his neck. His arms came around her and just held her until, in a matter of moments, the ache diminished. She sensed his tension and need for release, even as she felt his restraint in the bulging muscles of his arms. But she didn't want restraint. She wanted to experience it all.

"It's all right," she whispered. She wrapped her legs around his waist, drawing him deeper inside her. "I want to know everything."

He moaned, and she could almost feel his surrender. Then he drove into her. His breathing was a rough rasp in her ear, but the movement produced delicious sensations that made her heart race and her blood sing. She quickly learned the rhythm and moved with him. His urgency was contagious, fueling her own rising passion. The feelings were more powerful, more profound than she'd ever imagined. With Dawson, she rose higher and higher until bright light consumed her. Her world shattered into a thousand shards of glass.

As she drifted back to earth on a golden cloud, delicious aftershocks rippled through her. At the same time, Dawson strained, and she watched his face, the concentration in his features, the tension in his jaw. Then he lunged once more and stopped, groaning as he found release. Now that she knew the wondrous feeling herself, she was very happy to give to him in return.

Completely spent, Dawson lowered himself against her, then rolled to his back. He was still breathing hard. In the moonlight, she saw the astonishment mixed with anger on his face. She didn't understand. For several moments she watched him as he dragged air into his lungs.

"What's wrong?" she asked, pulling the sheet up over them.

"Why didn't you tell me you're a virgin?"

"I'm not."

"Don't be cute, Mattie. This isn't the time for cute. I suspected, but you told me about the jerk—when you were sixteen. I wasn't sure."

"I was merely calling a spade a spade. I am not a virgin."

"But you were until a couple of minutes ago."

She grinned. "What a wonderful thing. The world's oldest living virgin is now…not."

"This is serious," he snapped.

"I don't see why. We're both over twenty-one."

"One of us just barely," he said. There was self-loathing in his tone.

She ignored his comment and went on. "I'm an adult. I know my own mind. What's your problem?"

"For starters, I would have done it differently."

"Then I'm glad I didn't say anything, because I thought it was perfect." She turned to her side to look at him. "But for argument's sake, what would you have done differently?"

"Not that you deserve a response, but I would have gone more slowly. I would have taken the time to get you ready."

"I was ready. You don't get it, do you? I've been ready for years. Don't beat yourself up over it, Dawson." She frowned. "But I'm being selfish. Maybe *you* needed more time to get ready."

"Mattie, this is serious to me. Taking a woman's virginity is a responsibility. I guess I just wasn't prepared for exactly how inexperienced you are."

''I don't see what my experience or lack thereof has to do with anything. Sooner or later it has to go.''

''Right. To the man you marry. Now—''

''What are you saying, Dawson?''

Just then Mattie heard the hall door to the bedroom next door open. The light went on in the bathroom, and she heard a soft knock.

''Mattie, you awake? I heard you talking.''

Griff!

Before she could even sit up, the door swung open and her brother stood there backlit by the bathroom light. She was grateful that she couldn't see his expression.

When he charged the bed, Mattie was glad that she was closest to him.

Griff loomed over her, but he glared at Dawson. ''We had a deal. I told you to watch over my sister, not sleep with her yourself.''

''Hold on, Griff. This doesn't concern you,'' Dawson said.

Deal? Mattie went cold.

''The hell it doesn't concern me. Is this how you fulfill your responsibilities? When the cat's away...''

It was happening all over again, Mattie thought. It didn't matter that she was grown-up now. All the humiliation and pain she'd felt as a kid flooded her. She glanced at Dawson, who was watching her brother.

Griff glared at them for several moments, then said, ''I plan to break you in two, Prescott.''

Mattie already felt broken in two. Dawson was watching over her at Griff's command? That explained a lot, like why he'd been underfoot. And why he'd taken her to dinner. But the pain and betrayal were grinding through her. It was just like the last time. She had feelings for a guy. She acted on them. She got kicked in the teeth.

"You've got one minute, Prescott," Griff said, then turned on his heel and disappeared through the connecting bathroom.

Dawson pulled on briefs and slacks in about ten seconds flat, and followed, leaving Mattie alone in the bed. Anger closed in on her. He had only paid attention to her because Griff had intimidated him into the job. In essence, he'd hired a baby-sitter. She'd thought nothing could be worse than her humbling teenage experience. But this beat it by a mile. And she knew why.

She actually cared for Dawson.

If she hadn't, she wouldn't have slept with him. After sharing the intimacy, she now knew there was no way she could have done something so personal and private with just anyone.

It hurt deeply to know that Dawson had no feelings for her. To him it was probably nothing more than guard duty. Undercover work, so to speak. But the double entendre held no humor for her. After her makeover, when the cowboys had begun to take an interest in her, he must have stepped up surveillance, she realized. Making love had just been an assignment to him.

Her eyes burned with tears she wanted badly to let fall. But she wouldn't give him the satisfaction. She heard angry voices from the other room. She almost wished Griff would pop Dawson one. But no. Her brother was really furious. Dawson might actually get hurt.

Humiliated as she was, Mattie had no intention of being left out of this. Griff had no right to do anything.

He was out of bounds involving Dawson as bodyguard, and he had no business meting out punishment according to his own macho perception of right and wrong.

She threw the sheet back and jumped out of bed. After pulling on jeans and a shirt, she hurried through the connecting bath as the sound of male voices rose.

She walked into Griff's room, which was almost a duplicate of her own—double bed, distressed-wood dresser and nightstands, chair ottoman and table lamp in the corner and Western prints on the walls. Griff and Dawson stood at the foot of the bed. They were practically nose to nose, and were scowling at each other.

"This is all my fault," Dawson was saying. "Mattie's not to blame."

Anger pushed aside the pain she felt over his betrayal. "Why does anyone have to be blamed?" she asked. "We're consenting adults."

Neither man looked at her.

"I ought to tear you limb from limb," Griff ground out.

"Go ahead. It's no less than I deserve. But don't expect me to make it easy for you."

Mattie put her hands on her hips. "There will be no limb tearing."

They both ignored her.

"Dawson, what the hell were you thinking?" Griff poked his chest. "I guess the real question is which body part were you thinking *with?*"

Dawson smacked his hand away. "I take full responsibility for what happened."

Griff lifted his fists. "Damn right you'll take responsibility. I believe in justice, swift and sure."

"If you think it will solve something, I'm ready." Dawson widened his stance and bent his knees slightly.

That does it, Mattie thought.

She moved forward and insinuated herself between the two men. Size was on their side so she needed leverage. She rammed her shoulder into Griff and hit him somewhere in the chest area. He grunted as the wind was knocked out of him from the surprise attack. While she had him off balance, she put all her weight behind the move and drove him backwards a foot or so. When he regained his balance, he grabbed her shoulders. "Mattie, what the heck is wrong with you?"

"I'm getting sick and tired of people carrying on conversations about me right in front of me. As if I wasn't even here," she added for good measure. Her chest rose and fell rapidly from the force of her emotions and the effort of moving a man the size of her brother.

"I'll handle this, Mattie," Dawson said, putting his hands on her arms and gently moving her to the side, out of the way.

She rounded on him, glaring. Venting her rage felt wonderful. "Who do you think you are? You're a two-bit, low-down, underhanded, lying, scheming stuffed shirt!"

She looked at his bare chest and realized how wrong she was. He wasn't even *wearing* a shirt. It made her mad that she could notice the coarse dark hair across his muscular, masculine chest. She was madder still that he could affect her at all after what she'd found out.

"Mattie, calm down," he said. "I'm going to do the honorable thing."

"Damn right, you are," Griff growled. He moved to stand beside Dawson.

"I don't know what you're talking about, and I don't much care," she said. "Dawson and I did nothing wrong, Griff. You have no right to come in here like this. Like a—a Cro-Magnon man."

Griff still looked angry. "Mattie, I'm your brother. I love you, and it's my job to look out for you."

"Says who?"

"No one. But Reed is on his honeymoon and Brody is about to get married. That leaves me to take over. It's just understood."

"Well, I don't understand," she said. "And I've had enough. You've been butting into my love life ever since Frank Sinclair."

"Who's he?" Dawson asked with unmistakable menace in his voice.

Griff glanced at him. "He worked on the ranch when she was a kid. She had a crush on him. She told him how she felt, and he came to us. We made sure no one got close again." He glared at Dawson. "'Til now."

There was so much more that couldn't even be put into words. But thanks to the brothers Fortune, no man had gotten close since that day.

And no man had been able to take the sting out of the experience. Until now, she thought, echoing Griff's words as she looked at Dawson. She saw the pity in his eyes, and hated it.

"As mad as I am at you, Griffin Fortune, I do appreciate the fact that you care about me. But I will handle this."

"How?"

"What kind of a question is that?" she asked. "Just forget about it. What else is there to do?"

"Not damn likely we'll pretend it didn't happen," Griff said, meeting Dawson's look.

When the two men nodded slightly, Mattie wondered if there was some unspoken testosterone-fueled method of communication that only men understood.

"What do you mean?" she asked.

"You're going to marry him," Griff declared, just as Dawson said, "I'm going to marry you."

Nine

"Marry me? I've just discovered that you're the lying, cheating spawn of the devil—and you want to *marry* me?"

Dawson winced as the pitch in Mattie's voice escalated to a level that only he and dogs could hear. Not to mention the words *spawn of the devil*. How many times had he told himself he would never sink to the same level as his father? Before he could give that any more thought, she started to laugh. But there was a tinge of hysteria mixed in.

"I get it," she said, wiping her eyes. "Dawson, you're too much. Your first practical joke worked so well, you decided to try another one."

"What joke?" he asked.

"The one where you pretended to be interested in me while you were in cahoots with my brother to keep me from having any fun."

He met her gaze and willed her to understand. "Mattie, let's get one thing straight, here and now. I never pretend."

Especially about what had transpired between them tonight. He couldn't say for sure about her, but taking Mattie to bed had been the best thing he could remember in longer than he wanted to think about. Common sense told him that saying so in front of her brother would be a big mistake. He would lay money on the fact that Griff was mentally scrolling through his repertoire of three hundred ways to kill a man with his bare hands as he calculated the merits of each—as in, which one would hurt the most for the second-and-a-half it took Dawson to die.

Griff wasn't someone he wanted to make an enemy of. Which made him grateful that they were on the same wavelength. They both agreed on the issue of changing Mattie's marital status based on Dawson's participation in tonight's events.

She shook her head. "Maybe your term for it is 'play acting.' Whatever you want to call it, the fact is, it worked. Really well. But I guarantee you'll never sucker me again."

"It was no joke, Mattie. Not to me. In fact, I started to tell you what was going on, but you sidetracked me. And the bottom line is that now none of that matters. I want you to marry me."

"Why?" she asked.

"Because it's the right thing to do."

He winced for the second time in as many minutes. But this time it was because his words extinguished the light of expectation and hope in her eyes.

"Damn straight, it's right," Griff said. "And the sooner, the better." Obviously agitated, he ran a hand through his hair. "Since there's already a wedding in progress, maybe Brody and Jillian wouldn't mind making it a double—"

"Griff!" Mattie cried, glaring at him as if he were a wrestler asking to join a royal tea party. "This isn't a drink, and they aren't bartenders. Even if I wanted to—which I don't—I can't just walk up to Jillian and Brody and say 'make it a double.'"

Dawson wasn't so sure. He thought Griff's idea had

some value. Preparations were definitely going on. People were already planning to attend. The guest lists would be almost identical. Because of Jillian's pregnancy, she and Brody had decided to keep it small—mostly family and very close friends. Just a couple of days away, the date wouldn't give Mattie a chance to think this to death and then back out.

Once he convinced her to go along in the first place, of course.

Unfortunately, his mother was away and there wouldn't be time to get her here. But he would make it up to her. For as long as he could remember, he'd been making it up to her for the fact that his father had used her, then turned his back when he wanted a younger woman. And that's exactly the reason he was determined to marry Mattie. No one would ever have to make up to her for anything he had done. Unlike his father, Dawson would take responsibility for his actions. Period.

"A double wedding." Dawson nodded thoughtfully as he looked at the other man. "You may be on to something, Griff. I'll talk to Brody and see what he thinks. He and Jillian will be here in the morning for breakfast and a progress report on preparations for their wedding, anyway."

Griff nodded approval. "Good idea."

Mattie shook her head. "You guys are doing it again—talking as if I'm not here." She took her brother by the shirt front and pulled him down so they were nose to nose. "Read my lips. I'm not marrying Dawson or anyone else."

"Why not?" he asked. "I thought you wanted to get married and have a baby. Soon. Seems like it would be a good idea to make it legal." His eyes darkened and he never raised his voice, but there was no mistaking the threat there. "Since you already got a jump start on the baby part."

Good Lord, Dawson thought, he hadn't even considered *that* possibility. He had never been that irresponsible about birth control. But somehow where Mattie Fortune was concerned, all the rules went out the window, right along with his self-control.

But Griff was right. What if there was a baby? Even if there wasn't, Dawson had taken Mattie's virginity. Conscience and his personal code of honor dictated that he make an honest woman of her. He realized, though, that if he phrased it that way to her, he would need to duck and run.

"He's right, Mattie," Dawson said, taking the coward's way out and letting Griff's phrasing stand. "Like I said before, it's the right thing to do."

"For who? You keep saying it's right, but this is *not* the way my fantasy went."

"What fantasy?" Dawson asked.

She turned to him. "Ever since I was a little girl, I've dreamed of how it would be. Me. The man I love. A candlelight dinner. A proposal on bended knee accompanied by a declaration of undying love. When I pictured it, not even one of my brothers was there to spoil the moment. Siblings on deck sort of ruin the romance, if you know what I mean. This isn't even close to my daydream." Misery and betrayal brimmed in her eyes. She waved her hand dismissively. "Oh, look who I'm trying to reason with—Ugg and friend, the caveman conspiracy. I won't do it. You can't force me. Count me out. End of conversation," she said, and stalked back into her room.

Dawson went after her. Griff was right behind him.

Before Dawson could say anything, her brother started in. "You can't run away from this, Mattie."

"Says who?" She grabbed her denim jacket off the chair. "Watch me."

Griff took her arm in a gentle grip, but she couldn't break his hold without a struggle and probably not even then. "Not so fast," he said. "You're not going anywhere. Besides, I've got a question for you."

"Oh, yeah? What?"

"When I left Texas you were hardly more than a girl. Now you look like a woman. Who are you and what have you done with my little sister?" His tone was quiet and gruff, but unmistakably affectionate.

Dawson remembered asking her the same thing after her transformation. It occurred to him that her brother was seeing her for the first time since she'd changed her look *and* lost her virginity. It was a lot to absorb, and Dawson knew that if this were about his own sister, he would probably behave the same way as Griff.

Not to mention that buttering her up with flattery was a stroke of genius. For a secret-agent guy, Griff was okay in the diplomacy department. The question was, would it work?

Dawson was encouraged by the gradual, grudging softening in Mattie's expression.

"What do you mean?" she asked Griff.

"Your hair…" He shrugged, his gaze taking her in from head to toe. "I don't know. You just look different."

"Good or bad different?" There was skepticism in her tone.

"Good." He studied her, then nodded emphatically. "Definitely good different."

"Thank you." She reached both arms out and gave

him a big hug. "And I was very worried about you. I'm awfully glad that you're home safe and sound." She lowered her arms and stepped back. "Nice try, Griff. But it's not going to work. I still won't marry Dawson."

"Why the hell not?" Griff jammed his hands on his hips. "He slept with you, and he's willing to do the manly·thing and marry you."

"I slept with him, too. I'm doing the womanly thing and saying no. I have that right because I take just as much responsibility as he does. And I'm exercising my female prerogative to turn him down. Flat," she said, glaring first at her brother, then at Dawson.

Dawson scratched his head. Strike one for diplomacy. It was time for honesty. He looked at her brother. "Griff, could you give us a couple of minutes alone?"

"Why?" The other man looked like he would rather wrestle a five-hundred-pound alligator than leave any man alone with his little sister.

But at this point, it was sort of like closing the barn door after the horses got out. Judging by the scowl on the other man's face, Dawson decided, he'd better not point that out.

"I'd like to talk to her privately," he said. "This is something that concerns the two of us and I think we need some time to discuss where we go from here."

Glancing from Dawson to Mattie, Griff finally said warily, "Okay, but I'll be in the other room. Don't try to slip out the back, Prescott."

"The thought never entered my mind."

"If you need me, Mattie—"

"I won't," she interrupted.

After the doors between the two rooms were closed, Dawson said, "I understand why you're upset—"

"No, you don't," she said, shaking her head. "You don't have a clue what it feels like to be set up, then have the props knocked out from under you."

"Okay. Let's table the patronizing. I'll skip to the groveling part. I apologize for deceiving you, Mattie."

She sniffed. "From grovel to glib in the blink of an eye. You're good, Dawson."

He hadn't expected this to be easy, but she was really being stubborn. Probably because she'd been hurt before. Again, he wanted five minutes alone with the jerk who'd done this to her.

Knowing anger was unproductive, he tamped it down, making way for the guilt. Someone had hurt her, yet she'd given him a chance. And he'd betrayed her trust. Maybe if he tried to explain...

"Griff thought it was best that you didn't know he'd asked me to keep an eye on you. I agreed—reluctantly." He took in a deep breath. "In fact, I started to tell you tonight, before we—"

"Yeah," she said. Her cheeks turned pink with embarrassment. "I know what we did." Her voice was filled with self-recrimination.

That wasn't his intent. He would never want her to regret an experience that he'd found more satisfying—more wonderful—than anything he'd experienced in a long time. And he wasn't even sure why it had blown him away. Certainly not because she was accomplished at it, he thought wryly. But maybe that was her charm: the fact that it was her first time. Her innocence captivated him, along with the earthiness around the edges that was so appealing. Her zest for life was genuine and profoundly seductive.

The only thing he regretted was putting her in this position. Her brothers had kept her pure for the man she would marry. Now he would be that man.

He shook his head, trying to clear away the mental image of pure Mattie without a stitch of clothing, soft and sweet in his arms. He watched her, watching him as if she didn't believe a word that came out of his mouth. He would prove to her that he always meant what he said.

He rammed his fingers through his hair. "Although you probably won't believe this, I really was going to confess."

"Yeah, and next week I'm playing the harp for the San Antonio philharmonic."

"Sarcasm doesn't suit you, Matilda," he said.

She pointed at him. "I told you never to call me that."

"I remember. Because life as I know it would cease to exist. Here's a news flash—it already has."

"Well, there's a lot of that going around."

"I tried to tell you, Mattie. But I seem to remember you putting your hand over my mouth and doing some other things that distracted me." Her eyes widened slightly, and he was pretty sure she remembered the moment, too. "I don't expect you to admit it. The point is, I don't say anything I don't mean. And I mean to marry you. If you want a bended-knee proposal, I don't have a serious objection to that."

"No objection? Well, why didn't you say so before?" She raised one eyebrow. "Be still, my heart. Why do I feel like a potential client you're attempting to dazzle?" She held up her hand. "But let's leave that for a moment. A bended-knee proposal is small potatoes. What about the declaration of undying love?''

He squirmed. That was more complicated. ''Like I said, I won't lie to you. Dishonesty is not my style, even if I didn't care about you. Which I do. If I didn't—care about you, that is—we wouldn't be in this fix in the first place.''

She smiled, her full lips wavery. ''Be still, my heart,'' she said again. But the sardonic look disappeared, opening a small window to her hurt. Her voice softened. ''Somewhere in there I think I might have heard the world's smallest compliment.''

''But love—'' He ran a hand through his hair again and let out a long breath. ''I can tell you without hesitation that I respect you. I care about you. And after what I did, I refuse to walk away from you without making it right.''

''I'm mad as hell that you didn't tell me right away what Griff was up to.''

''You have every right to be,'' he said.

''I thought we tabled patronizing.''

''Sorry,'' he said sheepishly. He would have to learn not to underestimate her.

She tucked a strand of blond hair behind her ear. ''I appreciate the fact that you want to take responsibility. Truly I do. But don't you see, Dawson? I don't want to be anyone's responsibility. This should be the happiest day of my life. And it's not. Only that episode when I was sixteen takes a back seat to this.''

God, he hated topping the first jerk to hurt her. ''I'm sorry, Mattie. If I could change things, I would. But I have to ask, and I want you to really think about this. Will you marry me?''

"Don't think I'm an ungrateful wretch, but my answer has to be no."

Strike two for honesty.

The door opened and Griff stuck his head in. "You two have been talking in here for an awfully long time. What's the verdict, Dawson?"

He gave her brother a thumbs-down. "No go." It was time for reinforcements. "Griff, if you want to take a shot at convincing her, I wouldn't be offended."

"Well, I would," Mattie said. "Don't you guys know how to take no for an answer?" she asked.

"No," they said together.

For good measure, Griff stood in front of the door to his room, cutting off that escape route. Glancing over his shoulder, Dawson gauged the distance to the hall door and took two steps back to position himself so that she couldn't slip around behind him.

Dawson folded his arms over his chest. "Have at it, Griff."

The other man nodded. "Mattie," he began, "your brothers and I consider ourselves open-minded men." He ignored her rude, disbelieving sound and continued, "We understand that this sort of thing—"

"Define 'this sort of thing.'" There was a gleam in her eyes as she watched her brother squirm.

Dawson noted and admired Mattie's tenacious streak. She might be backed into a corner, but she wasn't going down by herself.

"You know. Sex," he mumbled. "It happens all the time with no strings attached."

"Since when are the lot of you understanding about me having sex?" she asked. "You guys have made it your mission in life to keep me pure as the driven snow."

"Until the right guy came along," Griff qualified.

"Or until I slept with one automatically qualifying him as Mr. Right," she shot back, sliding Dawson a look.

"Okay," Griff said, hands on hips as he nodded angrily. "I tried to reason with you, but it's time to get down and dirty."

More reinforcements? Dawson thought.

"What will your Mom and Dad think about this? Have you given that any thought?" Griff asked.

She looked stricken. It was the first chink in her armor that Dawson had ever seen. Some of the spirit seemed to drain out of her, and he hated being responsible for it. Apparently, there were some hurdles that stopped even Mattie Fortune dead in her tracks. He admired her devotion to family, while at the same time despising himself for going along with this to get what he wanted. To salve his own conscience. On his mental spreadsheet, he noted it in the Doing the Wrong Thing for the Right Reason column.

"Griff's right, Mattie. What do you think this will do to your parents?" he asked.

She caught her lower lip between her teeth and worried it as she thought. Finally she said, "They don't have to know."

"Do you really think they won't find out?" Griff asked.

"You wouldn't tell them," she scoffed.

"I will if I have to," her brother threatened. "Even if I didn't, your mother doesn't miss much. Halfway around the world as she is, she'll smell something fishy. She has a radar that would give air traffic controllers a run for their money."

Dawson thought about his own mother. He loved

her, but he couldn't say that she was particularly intuitive about him. Too bad. It might have been nice.

Mattie paced the room like a caged tigress. At one point, Dawson thought she was eyeing the window as an escape route, and he tensed, ready to stop her if need be. But she turned around and faced them both, head held high.

There was anger, hurt and violation in the stormy look she leveled at her brother and then at him. "If it were just to quiet the likes of you two, I would never in a million years agree to this. But you hit below the belt, Griff. Maybe that's why you're so good at whatever it is that you do on your secret trips."

"Mattie, I'm—"

"Stuff a sock in it. When you're right, you're right. Mom *will* know. Damn it."

Dawson didn't blame her for lashing out. This obviously hurt her a lot. The look in her eyes tied his gut in knots. If he could rewind the tape and fix things, he would do it in a flash. Since he couldn't, there was a part of him glad that she was weakening.

"I would rather die than do anything to cause my mother and father pain or worry or embarrassment. All right," she said looking at Dawson. "If the offer's still good, I'll marry you."

"The offer's still good," he said.

"Don't bother going down on one knee. We both know this isn't about me or what I want. It's not about love. It's about your overactive sense of honor. More's the pity," she said sadly.

From the moment he'd met her, Dawson had been trying to treat her as a child. Tonight she'd admitted to having girlish fantasies. But it gave him no satisfaction to discover that. He felt like the muck on the underside of a rock at the bottom of a lake. Not even a river where the garbage washed away. He was stagnant slime.

He'd singlehandedly been responsible for the death of her dream.

After a sleepless night, Mattie met her brother and his fiancé at the front door the following morning. She sent Brody to talk to Dawson and her uncle Ryan in the great room. With little or no coaxing, Mattie took Jillian on a tour of the outer courtyard where wedding preparations were under way. As they surveyed the outer adobe walls surrounding the stone patio, the fragrance of roses drifted to her. She breathed in the perfume, finding a small bit of comfort. This setting was idyllic: a garden filled with purple sage plants, ornamental grasses in shades of green and blue, roses and jasmine.

Mattie thought this a perfect place for her wedding. If Jillian agreed. Now it was time to broach the subject with her soon-to-be sister-in-law. She, Griff and Dawson had agreed to keep the reason behind the hurriedness of the marriage secret.

"I have an announcement to make," she said, nervously twisting her fingers together. Before Jillian could make a comment or even ask what, Mattie blurted out, "Dawson asked me to marry him, and I said yes."

Jillian's jaw dropped. She blinked a couple of times and finally said, "You and Dawson?"

"Yeah, I know it's sudden," Mattie answered, her cheeks burning. "But—"

"You and Dawson?"

"Strange, huh? I'm not sure I understand it myself. It just sort of happened."

"You and Dawson?"

Mattie glared at her. "Will you stop saying that?"

"I need to sit down," Jillian said. She lowered her pregnant fanny into the cushy pad on a wrought-iron chair that had been pushed to the side, making room for reception paraphernalia. She shook her head. "I knew you were up to something when you reinvented yourself."

"I what?"

The other woman waved her hand dismissively. "Oh, it's the politically correct term for getting a makeover. But I never in a million years guessed that you'd set your sights on Dawson Prescott. Or that you and Fortune's financial wizard had gotten so serious, so fast."

Numbers weren't the only thing he was a wizard at, Mattie thought, shivering at remembered pleasures from his gifted hands. How she wished she could tell her friend the truth. That she'd been pressured into this decision and was emotionally blackmailed into the marriage because she and Dawson had slept together. But she decided it was best to keep that detail to herself. She knew Jillian told Brody everything. Somehow it would get back to her mother and father. As soon as she worked up the courage, she would call home and tell them she was getting married. But she would spare them the ugly reality of why she was doing it.

How had the most wonderful night of her life landed her in the biggest mess of her life?

She plastered a sunny smile on her face and felt the ache start in her cheeks. She figured she'd best get used to it, since the next couple of days would be a repeat of what she was going through now. "It was love at first sight."

"Have you set a date?"

"Well, that's what I wanted to talk to you about. Since Dawson's sister and my brother Reed are going to be here for your wedding before going on to live in Australia, I was wondering—"

Jillian clapped her hands. "A double ceremony!"

Mentally, she breathed a sigh of relief that she was spared the asking. "I don't want you to feel you have to say yes."

"Of course not."

"We just thought it might be advantageous—"

"Convenience shouldn't be a consideration when you're talking about love," Jillian scolded good-naturedly.

If they were talking about love, Mattie would have agreed with her. But this whole thing came under the heading of Suffering the Consequences of Your Actions. And *suffering* was the key word.

She just couldn't quite figure out why Dawson was doing it. Griff was intimidating, but the instincts she relied on with her horses told her that her fiancé wasn't afraid of her brother. So what was his reason for going through with this farce of a marriage?

"I think it's a great idea," Jillian said.

"Really? You wouldn't feel as if you're having to share the limelight?"

"I love the idea of sharing the limelight with you."

"You're sure you wouldn't hate me forever?" Mattie met her gaze squarely. "Before you answer, think very carefully."

"I don't have to think carefully. My answer is that

it will be twice as wonderful for Brody and me if you and Dawson join in our happiness.''

Mattie breathed a sigh. ''All right. Then it's settled—''

''I just thought of something. We'll have the same anniversary.''

Mattie's head was spinning from everything she'd thought about. ''That's true.''

''Oh, no,'' Jillian said. ''I just thought of something else. And this is a potential problem.''

After what she'd been through, Mattie couldn't take another problem—potential, implied or real. ''What?'' she asked, tensing.

''You're supposed to be my bridesmaid. How can you be a bride at the same time?''

Breathing a sigh of relief, Mattie shook her head. ''I don't see any problem. We'll just stand up together and take vows one at a time.''

''But your bridesmaid's dress is green velvet for my ceremony. Don't you want to wear traditional white for yours?''

Nothing about this was traditional, Mattie thought as profound sadness and anger twisted together inside her. She almost blurted that out to Jillian, but kept it to herself. The last thing she wanted to do was spoil her friend's happy day. She and Brody had waited a long time and gone through a lot finally to be together. No way would Mattie rain on their parade.

She sat on the brick step beside her friend and rested her hands on Jillian's chair arm, her chin on her linked fingers. ''How about this?'' she asked. ''You and Brody take your vows first. We'll go through the whole ceremony, take pictures, everything. I'll disappear to change into my...traditional wedding outfit.

While I'm doing that, my uncle can make an announcement that there will be another wedding. It will be like two separate ceremonies, but we'll share guests and a reception.''

"That's a wonderful idea," Jillian said.

"Are you sure it's all right with you?"

"I'm positive." Jillian's face brightened even more as she spotted Brody and Dawson approaching. "Look who's here. Speak of the devils.''

"You got that right," Mattie said under her breath as she watched her fiancé walk toward them.

"What did you say?" Jillian asked.

"I said, 'What a sight we'll be.'''

When the men joined them, Mattie noted the sparkle of anticipation in Brody's eyes as he leaned down to kiss his wife-to-be. He caressed her rounded belly tenderly. "How are you?" he asked.

"Fine and dandy." Jillian smiled lovingly at him.

Mattie looked at Dawson and wondered what he was thinking as he watched the devoted couple. His look gave nothing away. "So how did it go with Uncle Ryan?" she asked as brightly as she could.

"You mean, when I asked him for your hand in marriage?" Dawson said.

"Is that what you did?" she asked.

Studying his expression, she did not find even a trace of humor. He was completely serious. There was something so old-fashioned and courtly about the gesture of asking permission from the senior male in the family that it warmed her heart. The whole affair seemed so passionless and she needed so badly to discover some hint of warmth, spirit, meaning—soul.

"You asked Uncle Ryan for permission to marry me?" she repeated.

"He sure did." Brody grinned. "Said that since Dad and Mom are so far away, Ryan is the next in line, and he asked permission to make you his wife."

"And?" Mattie asked.

Brody shrugged. "You're over twenty-one. What was he going to say?"

"It's about darn time." Mattie threw up her hands. "I've been trying for ages to make everyone recognize that I'm a mature woman."

"He also said that he will pull strings and call in favors if necessary to push through the paperwork for a marriage license," Dawson replied.

Brody kissed her cheek. "Congratulations, sis. Dawson's a good man. This is pretty sudden, but when it's right, it's right. No point in fighting it. Jillian and I tried that and it didn't work."

Mattie narrowed her gaze on Dawson and wondered what he'd said to her brother. How had he convinced him it was right? Somehow she had a sneaking suspicion that it was practically word for word what she'd told Jillian. And for the same reason—to preserve the happiness of their day.

"Yes, indeed," she said. "Three days from now we'll all be saying, 'I do.'"

Ten

Clutching her bouquet of baby's breath, carnations and marigolds, Mattie stood in the great room and looked through the French doors to the courtyard that was filling with guests. Everyone was waiting until stragglers arrived for the one o'clock wedding and were seated. Then Brody and Jillian's ceremony would start. She looked at the cloudless blue sky in the distance and was grateful that it was a beautiful day for a wedding. And that her parents wouldn't witness her wedding, what would not be her happiest day.

They had practically just returned to Australia from Reed and Mallory's nuptials. Brody and Jillian planned to visit when they could after the baby was born. Although a little sad, Mattie was relieved too. Her mother would see through her like no one else could.

That was one less thing to worry about.

Three days earlier, Mattie hadn't been prepared for the level of terror that awaited her in this spot. So many kinds of terror, too. Like high heels. She glanced down at the hunter-green satin toes of her shoes that matched her velvet bridesmaid's dress. She was used to jeans and boots. What if she tripped walking between the rows of chairs where the guests sat? What if the crown of flowers encircling her head fell off while the ceremony was going on? What if she had a coughing attack? Or worse, a sneeze, and her nose started to run? What if she embarrassed her brother on the most important day of his life?

And that was just for starters. Then came the part when it would be the biggest day of *her* life.

Which brought her down her long list of terrors to Dawson Prescott. Or, more specifically, to marrying him. She was almost grateful to the terror that pumped adrenaline through her, because she'd hardly slept in three days. At least the panic kept her eyes open.

She had the strongest urge to run far and fast, but two things stopped her. No way would she let Brody and Jillian down and spoil their special day. Although she supposed she could go through their ceremony and then run like hell. But that wouldn't work because no way would she let her parents down, either. As Dawson would say, that was "unacceptable."

"How are you doing?"

Dawson. Without turning around, Mattie knew it was him. She knew his calm, steady voice, so deep that it raised tingles on her skin from head to toe. He stood behind her, so close that she could smell the intoxicating scent of his aftershave, hear his even breathing, feel the warmth from his body. Part of her wanted to savor it, wrap herself in it because she was cold from the inside out. Part of her wanted to tell him to back off because he was the reason she was cold.

But she didn't say anything. Later he would get what he deserved.

She turned around and was unprepared for the spectacular view of him in a traditional black tuxedo, white, pleated dress shirt with black studs marching down his chest, and bow tie, perfectly knotted at his neck. His sun-streaked hair was neatly combed. He was so handsome that he took her breath away. Not only that, but for a few moments she completely forgot to be mad at him.

There was a gleam in his eyes as he looked her over, from the top of her head, down the length of her dress, to the tips of her shoes peeking out from beneath her hem. His gaze met hers and there was an intensity in it that sent excitement skimming through her.

"You look beautiful," he said, his voice a shade huskier than just a moment before.

"So do you," she blurted out.

"Thanks." He grinned, and her heart started tap dancing.

"Don't let it go to your head," she grumbled, reminding herself that she was not happy with him. "I'm sure it's the clothes."

"You're still mad." It wasn't a question.

She shrugged. "Even if I wasn't, I still think it's the clothes."

"Is Jillian ready?" he asked, apparently deciding to retreat.

Mattie nodded. "Amy's with her." At his blank look, she said, "Amy Fairaday, Jillian's sister. She's the maid of honor and seems to be doing a fine job of keeping the bride calm."

"That's good," he said.

"Yup. Jill is as cool as a cucumber." She looked at him and realized he looked pretty cool, too, in view of what they faced. Then she wondered about her brother. "What about Brody?"

"Reed is with him, since he's the best man. I picked him and Mallory up at the airport this morning and brought them here, to the ranch. Since I had to be here anyway."

She ignored his casual reference to their impending nuptials. She didn't want to think about it until it was absolutely necessary. "Did they have a good trip?" She avoided using the word *honeymoon*. It would evoke too many erotic images that she couldn't deal with at the moment. She was already in hot water herself for putting the "wedding night" before the wedding.

"They said their honeymoon couldn't have been more perfect."

So much for avoiding the word. Leave it to Dawson. She was about to ask if he'd said anything to her brother and his sister about their surprise, when there was a commotion behind them. Jillian moved through the great room, decked out in her wedding finery and looking more beautiful than Mattie had ever seen her. She'd opted for a simple, floor-length, cream-colored dress with loose lines that minimized the appearance of her pregnancy. Her veil was anchored by a halo wreath of flowers in her straight, shoulder-length blond hair. The look was uncomplicated, yet delicately feminine.

Her sister was beside her. Amy was a little taller than Jillian, with the same coloring, blond and beautiful. "Brody has taken his place in the courtyard beside the justice of the peace. I think we're ready to start, sis," she said. She looked at the assembled group like a general surveying his troops. "Everyone know what to do? Mattie and Dawson go first."

Mattie nodded, even as her heart pounded so hard she thought it might pop from her chest. During rehearsal the night before, it had been decided that ushers and bridesmaids would walk together down the aisle.

Dawson cleared his throat. "Break a leg, kid."

"Oh, Lord, I hope not," she cried.

"It's just an expression. It means 'Good luck.'"

"I knew that," she said.

He held out his arm, and Mattie placed her shaking hand in the bend of his elbow. When he reached out and covered her cold fingers with his warm palm, she found the gesture surprisingly comforting. Mattie would have denied it from one end of the huge state of Texas to the other, but she was terribly grateful for Dawson's presence. She gripped her bouquet in her other hand and nodded that she was ready.

"Let's go," he said, opening the French doors.

He signaled to the quartet of musicians in the far corner of the courtyard. Instantly they stopped the chamber music they'd been playing, adjusted the sheet music on their stands, and started the traditional wedding march. The guests swiveled in their chairs to watch the procession, all of them smiling indulgently.

As she walked by, Mattie saw Dawson's sister, Mallory, and didn't miss the surprised look on her face. At first she wondered if her bra strap were showing, or if there were a spot on her dress. She stumbled slightly and felt Dawson's arm tense as he slowed to let her regain her balance.

Dawson bent and whispered in her ear. "Mallory hasn't seen you since the transformation."

She nodded, grateful for his support, yet at the same time angry that she was grateful to him for anything. She looked at him, trying to read the expression in his hazel eyes. Was he thinking about the fact that a little while from now, the two of them would be taking this same walk to become man and wife?

Before she could give that too much thought, they

reached the flower-covered arch where her two brothers stood beside the justice of the peace dressed in a black robe. She released Dawson's arm and walked to the left, while he took his place beside the groom and best man on the right. She turned and watched the rest of the bridal procession.

She quickly glanced at Jillian, then swung her gaze to see the look on Brody's face. Her heart caught at the look of admiration, awe, wonder, and most of all love, that was in his eyes. Then a feeling of sadness enveloped her. How she'd always hoped that the man she married would look at her like that.

But it wasn't to be.

When the bridal couple were together in front of the arbor, arm in arm, the ceremony began. Different friends and relatives that Jillian and Brody had chosen ahead of time read inspirational pieces about devotion, love, soul mates, and happily-ever-after. Each one was like a knife through Mattie's heart.

Finally, the bride and groom faced each other and joined hands. They each made promises that they'd written themselves. Then the justice of the peace had them repeat the traditional vows to love, honor and cherish. Finally, he beamed at Brody and said, "You may kiss your bride."

"With pleasure," Brody said. He molded Jillian against him with one arm, then cupped her cheek with his hand and lowered his mouth to hers. The kiss seemed to go on and on, until hoots and catcalls from the guests forced the laughing couple to separate.

"Ladies and gentlemen," the judge said, "may I present to you Mr. and Mrs. Brody Fortune."

Applause filled the courtyard. Sadness and guilt filled Mattie's heart. She was glad her brother and Jillian had finally found each other. At the same time, she was so envious of their happiness that she could hardly stand it. It was such a stark contrast to the punishment she faced of marrying a man who didn't love her.

Jillian and Brody walked back among their guests. Amy took Reed's arm and moved away from the arbor. Then Dawson was beside her, and she felt the rush of hummingbird wings inside her that she was beginning to associate with his closeness. As they entered the house, she heard the judge, still standing in front of the arbor, ask for everyone's attention. He asked the guests to stay in their seats; he had a surprise announcement from the family. When he finished, voices rose to an excited buzz.

Here it comes, she thought. *My turn.* With every ounce of willpower in her body, she held back the tears that burned her eyes.

Dawson stood beside the justice of the peace, waiting for Mattie to open the French doors and walk down the aisle to join him. Griff had agreed to be his best man, mostly, Dawson was sure, to make certain they went through with the wedding.

Scanning the gathered guests, he spotted Mallory. After he'd brought her to the ranch from the airport, he'd confided to her that he was getting married. He'd braced himself for her attempt to talk him out of making the biggest mistake of his life. Surprisingly, she'd hugged him and said she wasn't shocked in the least. With all the sparks he and Mattie had set off the first time they'd laid eyes on each other, it had been a good thing it wasn't raining. Everyone at that rodeo would have been electrocuted by their love at first sight.

Sparks? Love at first sight?

Dawson didn't believe in it. But if romantic notions kept his sister happy, far be it from him to set her straight. Suddenly he felt Griff stiffen, and he looked up in time to see Willa Simms come through the French doors.

"I didn't know Mattie asked Willa to stand up with her," Griff whispered to him.

Dawson met his gaze. "Probably because Mattie is giving you the silent treatment."

"True enough." He nodded grimly. "Did you know about Willa?"

"Mattie's giving me the silent treatment too," he said. "I knew they became friends while both of them were here on the ranch. But the renovations on her apartment in College Station were completed and recently she moved in. I didn't know Mattie had talked to her."

"When did Willa move?"

Dawson shrugged. "About a week ago, I guess."

"She's not wearing her glasses," Griff observed.

Dawson studied her. In her ankle-length peach gown with matching jacket, she looked very pretty. Her auburn hair was pulled up at the crown, and curls spilled down, with wisps framing her face. She smiled shyly as she walked. When she reached the arbor, her gaze was on Griff, and there was a sparkle in her eyes. The judge indicated where she should stand, since she hadn't been there for the previous evening's rehearsal.

Then Dawson fixed his gaze on the French doors. Knowing how close she was to her family, he felt badly that this had moved too quickly for them to come. On the other hand, they were protected from details he would rather they not know. His heart

pounded as he waited expectantly for Mattie. He didn't
know how she could top the beautiful picture she'd
made in her bridesmaid's dress. She had bowled him
over. But he found that the thought of seeing her walk
gracefully toward him to become his wife made his
palms sweat and his heart race.

When she appeared in the doorway, Dawson was
stunned. Instead of the white dress and veil he'd expected, she was wearing her jeans, boots and denim
shirt. The guests whispered to each other, replacing
the astonished silence her appearance had caused.
With chin held high, she moved down the aisle, a
smile plastered on her face. The seductive sway of her
hips kicked his heart into double time. His gaze lowered to the shapely curves of her thighs and calves.
Not until that moment had he realized how much he'd
missed the sight of her long, slender legs, which had
been hidden by her floor-length dress.

When she reached him, they assumed their places
before the judge, who removed the glasses from his
nose and stared at her. "I thought you were going to
change," he said.

"Yes, sir. I did."

"For your wedding," he added.

"I know," she answered, nodding.

"But you're wearing jeans." The justice of the
peace gazed from the toes of her scuffed boots to her
jeans. They were so worn and soft that they were almost threadbare at the pressure points, Dawson noted,
which also happened to be where she was curvy. The
thought made his mouth go dry and his blood pressure
jump a couple of notches.

"Your Honor, I train horses for a living. This is
who I really am." She angled her head toward Daw-

son. "Makeup and a fancy dress got his attention. But he needs to know what he's getting into."

The judge sighed. "My wife would say that marriage to a man is a lot like training a horse," he said.

She grinned. "I'm glad you see my point."

"Although some take to the reins better than others," he added, glancing at Dawson.

"Remember what they say," Dawson interjected.

"What's that?" Mattie and the judge asked in unison.

"You can't teach an *old* dog new tricks." Dawson knew she got the double meaning, even if the judge didn't.

Mattie glared at him as he took her hand, but didn't pull away. Instead she whispered, "Make no mistake, Dawson, you can't make a silk purse from a sow's ear. What you see is what you get."

"Okay."

She looked momentarily taken aback. "So you still want to go through with this?"

"Absolutely. I wouldn't change a hair on your head or anything else about you," he said, glancing down at her denim shirt, at the point where the snaps closed just above her breasts.

He'd been half kidding, but Dawson was surprised to realize that what he'd told her was true. In front of God and everyone present, she'd made it clear what her feelings were. He admired her fearless spirit and total honesty. He also saw the insecurity lurking in her eyes. She wasn't as tough as she pretended. He would do his best to protect her tender heart from hurt.

"All right, then," she said. "Let's get this show on the road."

The judge cleared his throat. "Dearly beloved, we

are still gathered before God to unite *this* man and *this* woman in holy matrimony.''

''Can we just skip to the 'I dos?''' Mattie asked him.

The judge raised one white eyebrow. ''You don't want all the trimmings?''

''Do I look like an all-the-trimmings kind of woman?''

He gave her attire another once-over and sighed. ''Good point.'' He met Dawson's gaze and shook his head sympathetically. ''Son, you've got your work cut out for you.''

''Truer words were never spoken,'' Dawson said.

''What about me?'' she asked indignantly. ''Don't you think I've got my work cut out for me? Haven't you ever heard the saying— You can't judge a dog by its spots? Your Honor, you don't know what a trial *he* can be,'' she said, cocking her thumb in Dawson's direction. Then she realized what she'd said and chuckled at her pun. ''A little legal humor.''

The justice looked taken aback. ''Frankly, I'm not exactly sure what to think about the two of you. As a favor to your uncle Ryan, I'm not going to walk out. So let's do this wedding before I change my mind.''

''She'll behave,'' Dawson said, hoping it was true. He knew her behavior was calculated to make him change his mind. If anything, it made him want her more. For the life of him, he hadn't a clue why.

The judge looked at them sternly, then said, ''Do you, Dawson Geoffrey Prescott—''

''Geoffrey?'' Mattie whispered.

''My father's name,'' Dawson whispered.

He couldn't help thinking how appropriate it was to have a reminder of his reasons for marrying Mattie.

He might have his father's name, but no way was he as unfeeling and irresponsible as the man whose blood ran through his veins.

"—take this woman for your lawful wife," the judge continued, ignoring their exchange.

"I do," Dawson said, loudly and clearly.

"Do you Matilda Theodora—"

"Theodora?" Dawson repeated, raising an eyebrow.

"My father's name," she said.

"—take this man," the judge continued, frowning at them as if they were two recalcitrant children.

"I do." She mumbled something else that sounded an awful lot like *under protest,* But Dawson knew no one else could hear it and it was for his ears alone.

The judge looked at them over the glasses perched on the end of his nose and said, "Then with the authority granted to me by the glorious state of Texas, I pronounce you husband and wife." He met Dawson's gaze. "And may God have mercy on you."

"Amen to that," Dawson said. Then he took Mattie in his arms and thoroughly kissed his bride as he'd been wanting to all day.

Dawson and Mattie were in the study with Ryan, Griff and Willa. While her aunt Lily was seeing to the guests at the reception, they were gathered to make sure the wedding paperwork was in order before the judge left.

Now her uncle handed each of them a glass of champagne. "I propose a toast," he said. "To Dawson, a man I've come to think of as a son. Now you're officially a member of the family. And my niece, Mattie. In a short time, you've become more like a daughter to me. May your life together be filled with adventure, laughter, and most of all, love.''

"To Mattie and Dawson," they chorused.

As Mattie sipped, she thought about her uncle's toast. Adventure was good. Laughter, probably. She figured she and Dawson might be able to manage that. His reaction to her wedding attire had encouraged her on that score. He looked very surprised but not at all angry or upset, as she'd expected. Amused was more how she would describe his response. But love? She hoped so.

At least on Dawson's part. She studied Dawson, so handsome in his tuxedo. Her pulse quickened as she observed his square jaw and wide shoulders. Yet there was gentleness in him as he held the crystal flute. And the way he'd made love to her... So considerate. And he'd been angry that she hadn't told him she was a virgin so that he could have taken better care. The thought started a glow in the center of her abdomen and radiated outward.

Now they were husband and wife, and it was legal to make love anytime. Anticipation filled her at the idea of being close to him again.

More than that, she planned to do her best to find love with him. The only way she'd been able to force herself to walk down that aisle was her determination to try and make him love her. She realized that her prank attire probably hadn't been putting her best boot forward. But his response had encouraged her. Maybe he wasn't as much of a stuffed shirt as she'd thought. And if she tried very hard, she could be his helpmate in life. Maybe love would follow.

Dawson held up his glass. "My thanks to Griff for being my best man.''

"You're welcome," Griff answered gruffly. "I wouldn't have put on this monkey suit for anyone but Mattie."

If he hadn't meddled, she thought, he wouldn't have had to dress up at all. Sniffing over his attempt at diplomacy, Mattie held up her glass. "I propose a toast to Willa. Thanks for standing up with me on such short notice."

Willa tucked a strand of auburn hair behind her ear and clinked Mattie's glass. "It was my pleasure. I'm so happy to be included in all your family gatherings. Dad and Ryan became best friends in Vietnam. Since my father passed away two years ago, I've missed him terribly. He would be happy knowing I'm not alone. It's wonderful to be around people." She glanced shyly at Griff.

Well, well, Mattie thought. *She's got an eye for my brother. The big lug doesn't deserve her.* At least not until Mattie got over being mad at him for forcing Dawson to marry her. How long would it take before she would forgive him? As long as it took for Dawson to fall in love with her. And that could take a very long time.

Mattie pushed aside her feelings and smiled at Willa. "You're like family, Willa. So tell me about your apartment. Is the redecorating completed?"

The other woman sipped thoughtfully and nodded. "It's fine. I love the area and can't wait to start teaching."

Mattie thought she detected some reserve in her friend, and wondered if she should say anything. "Well, I'm glad. And especially grateful that you could be here with me today."

"I'm glad you called me."

"That reminds me," Mattie said. Things had been a whirlwind and she had forgotten to bring up something that had bothered her since that call to her friend. She decided to say something, and they could all tell her she was a worrywart. "You sounded funny the other night when we talked on the phone. Is everything all right?"

Willa nodded, a bit too emphatically. "Fine. It's just…"

"What?" Griff asked, a note of concern in his voice.

Mattie frowned. Her brother, too, sensed that something wasn't quite right with Willa.

The other woman shrugged. "When Mattie called, I almost didn't answer."

"Why?" Griff said, the concern cranking up a notch.

"It's too stupid to bring up."

Uncle Ryan sipped his champagne. "Nothing is too stupid to bring up. Especially while Clint Lockhart is still at large."

"I've been getting calls." Willa shrugged. "But I'm just being a baby. It's a new place. I'm all by myself. Strange sounds. I just have to get used to it."

"Maybe," Dawson said. "But Ryan's right. With Clint out there, you can't be too careful."

"What kind of calls?" Griff asked.

She looked at the three men, anxiety in her blue-gray eyes. "Hang-ups all times of the day and night. It's the ones that wake me from a sound sleep that are the most disturbing. I can hear someone breathing on the other end of the phone, but no one says anything."

Ryan put his glass on the desk. "Damn it. Clint Lockhart."

"Are you sure it's a man?" Dawson asked.

"I have no idea." Willa shook her head. "No one ever says anything."

"It's Clint. He hasn't been apprehended," Ryan said, his words humming with anger. "I talked to Sheriff Grayhawk before the wedding. Clint's eluded law enforcement, just dropped out of sight. They think someone's hiding him."

"But how would he know where Willa lives? And why would he target her, anyway?" Mattie asked.

"Who knows how he finds out anything?" Ryan answered, his voice curt with frustration. "As far as targets, his mind is so whacked, I don't think he's discriminating. He wants to get me. He'll do that by hurting anyone I care about. Security here on the ranch is tight, and he can't get to anyone here. So…" He shrugged, letting the disturbing thought spin out.

Mattie noticed that Griff shifted closer to Willa when the other woman shivered at the words.

Ryan looked at Griff. "I want you to do a security check on Willa's phone and the rest of her apartment."

Griff moved his shoulders restlessly, as if he wasn't comfortable in his own skin. "Yes, sir. But are you sure I'm the right man—"

"You're a Fortune. You're the best at your job." Ryan nodded. "I can trust you with my godchild's safety. You're definitely the right man."

Willa's cheeks turned a becoming shade of pink. "Are you sure that's necessary? I don't think Clint would do anything to me."

Ryan shook his head angrily. "Until he's behind bars again, the whole Fortune family is at risk." He looked at Dawson. "That goes for you, too. Mattie's your responsibility now. My niece's safety is in your hands. She's your wife.''

"I'll take good care of her, sir," Dawson said.

His wife. Mattie shivered at the thought.

"Good." Ryan walked to the door. "I suggest we go out and mingle with everyone. Jillian and Brody planned to stay for a little while, then head out on their honeymoon. Don't want to miss them." He looked from Dawson to Mattie, who squirmed under his look. "What about you two? Any plans for a trip?''

Dawson glanced at her as he hesitated a moment. She refused to jump in and help him. This was his idea; he could field the difficult questions.

Finally he said, "Mattie and I had such a whirlwind courtship, and jumping into the wedding while Mallory and Reed were still here in the States, we want to catch our breath. We'll take our time and think about a honeymoon.''

Good save, Dawson, she thought. She had to give him credit. He was smooth.

"Sounds wise," Ryan said as he walked through the doorway.

Willa and Dawson followed him. Mattie started after them, but Griff stopped her with a hand on her arm. "Mattie, I'm not sure I can handle the security job at Willa's.''

"Why?''

There was worry in his brown eyes, making them darker than usual; his lips tightened as he looked at her. "She's such a lady. And I'm—'' He shrugged. "You know, rough around the edges. I think Ryan should find someone else to check out her place.''

The vulnerability Mattie saw in his eyes punctured

her bubble of anger, which flew off like a deflating balloon. She touched his arm. "You're exactly the right man to do the job—for all the reasons Uncle Ryan said. Besides, I think Willa's got a crush on you."

He reached out and felt her forehead. "No fever. Guess marriage has already done a number on you."

She laughed. "Okay. Don't listen to me. But you're right about marriage. It's a scary proposition."

Griff encircled her shoulders and pulled her against him in a quick hug. "I have a feeling everything is going to work out fine."

"From your mouth to God's ear," she whispered fervently.

The thought of being Mrs. Dawson Prescott brought to mind a whole lot of apprehension. It had nothing to do with Clint Lockhart—and everything to do with whether or not she could find love with her husband.

Eleven

Dawson stopped his BMW at the gate to his Kingston Estates home, lowered the driver's window and punched several buttons on a keypad. The next thing Mattie knew, the wrought-iron gate, part of the brick-capped wall that surrounded his property, whispered open.

"This is it," he said, guiding the car up the long drive that curved to the left before stopping in front of the house. There was unmistakable pride in his voice, and from the little she could see of the impressive structure in the dark, he had every right to feel that way.

"It's really something," she answered.

Mattie was almost grateful for not sleeping much since becoming engaged to Dawson. Lack of rest, combined with nonstop wedding preparations had made her numb. She wasn't sure how to feel, which was probably a good thing. She was almost beyond feeling anything at all. The clock on the car's dashboard showed midnight. The optimum hour to begin her fairy tale. Or end it.

She would assume her role as Dawson's wife—with all the fringe benefits. Like sharing his bed. The thought made her shiver with anticipation, and she realized that maybe she wasn't as tired as she'd thought.

Another blissful night in his arms would make all the stress worth it.

He turned the car's ignition off and the engine died, along with the interior dash lights. She glanced to her right and noticed that the planters across the whole front of the house, including the walkway, were rimmed with small lights.

"I never saw lights with little hats on before," she said. "They're cute."

He got out of the car and walked around to her side, looking tense in the dim light from the open door. "I'm glad you like them, but cute isn't their primary function."

"Heaven forbid they're just decorative. What might their primary function be?"

"This lot is two acres, and the house is set pretty far back, away from the street and the lights. The cute little guys illuminate the walkway so you don't trip and break your neck," he answered. He didn't sound angry, so much as tired and uptight.

"And a worthy service they provide," she agreed.

Dawson opened the trunk and lifted out the several suitcases she'd packed. They had agreed she would get the rest of her things from the ranch later. He hefted her bags and led the way past the house's stonework facade up the steps to the raised-panel oak door. Leaded, beveled glass decorated the center panel. With interior lights on, this door would be breathtakingly beautiful, she thought as Dawson unlocked and opened it.

He reached past her and flipped on the entryway light, then let her precede him into the house. The odor of fresh paint tickled her nose. At least he hadn't lied to her about that.

But as she surveyed her new home, something about the place left her vaguely uneasy. She couldn't put a finger on why.

"The house is trilevel," Dawson explained.

They had walked straight into the living room, which had high ceilings and a bay window. He led her up a half-flight of stairs. "This is the formal dining room, kitchen and family room." He set her bags down there.

"It's beautiful," she said, meaning it. She walked past the huge oak table and hutch in the dining room and leaned over the oak railing to peer down into the living room. "Really impressive," she said.

But something about it still disturbed her.

She met him in the family room, where the furniture consisted of a leather couch and love seat set at a right angle to each other. They were arranged in front of the brick fireplace. Lamps were made of wrought-iron and wood. In spite of the expensive furnishings, the room felt spartan, without pictures on the walls or framed photographs on the mantel. In the corner of the vast area sat the biggest television set she had ever seen. The ceiling was dotted with grids that she assumed were speakers for a sound system.

Dawson apparently noticed where she was looking. "State-of-the-art surround sound," he said proudly. "It will make you feel like you're at the movies."

"Lovely," she answered. "Vibrating from the outside in."

"The master bedroom is this way," he said, pointing down the hall before leading the way.

Her heart started to pound as she followed. *The bedroom I will share with my husband.* He flipped on the light, illuminating a huge room dominated by a king-size bed covered with a black comforter. The oak headboard reminded Mattie of an entertainment center and took up almost one wall. It was a series of sliding doors, drawers and cupboards. In her fairy tale, the bed had always been a megaromantic four-poster. Except when she was about seventeen and she thought waterbeds were the best thing since sliced bread. But this bed was certainly big enough for a married couple to explore each other. She shivered with excitement.

The bathroom had two sinks with gold fixtures, and a stall shower. What fascinated her most was the whirlpool bath, which looked as if it would hold the two of them very comfortably, even though Dawson was a big man. The thought sent a flash-fire of sensation sweeping over her body. The walk-in closet was the size of a bedroom and was filled with Dawson's suits, ties, dress shirts, shoes, jeans and boots. Big as it was, all the hanging space was used.

He showed her two more bedrooms. One was set up with a computer desk, fax machine, copy machine, and telephones—obviously a home office. The other had gym equipment—weight bench, exercise cycle, treadmill, and other gizmos with weights, cables and handles that looked to her like torture devices left over from the Spanish Inquisition.

Next he led her to the bottom and final level of the house. It featured a great room with more leather furniture, a spare room for storage, and another bedroom that opened onto the brick-trimmed patio and pool area.

After showing her everything, Dawson led the way back up the half-flight of stairs to the family room. He rested his hands on his hips and swung his gaze around the room proudly.

"So what do you think of it?" he asked.

"I think the floor plan is wonderful," she answered sincerely. But the whole place left her feeling cold and unwelcome. Every room he'd shown her had made her more and more uneasy. But why? "The rooms are large with lots of windows. It's huge."

"So which bedroom do you want?" he asked.

Uh-oh. "What did you say?" she asked, unable to believe her ears.

"I asked which room you want. The way the house is laid out, it's like having two master suites. Since they're on separate floors, we can both have our privacy."

She stared at him. "Privacy?"

Disappointment filled her. She'd always thought married people slept in the same room. Her parents did. Uncle Ryan and Aunt Lily did. She'd bet her favorite saddle that none of her married brothers, and even the ones who *weren't* hitched, slept in a bed separate from their significant other. Her one and only experience had shown her it was one of the marriage perks.

"Privacy?" she asked again.

"Yeah. The master gives you kitchen privileges. But downstairs is easily accessible to the pool and whirlpool bath outside. Both floors have a family room. It will work out great."

Great if you want to avoid someone, she thought. *Great if you want to dodge, elude, escape or flee from the woman you just married. Great if you want privacy.*

Finally she got what had been bothering her since walking into his house. The unmistakable signs of new paint were there. The rest of the house shouted No

Women Allowed. He didn't want a wife. He didn't want a woman to share his life. He didn't want to be married. In fact, he looked as miserable as she felt.

She might have worked up some pity for him, except she had the unshakable sense that even if Griff hadn't pushed the issue, Dawson would have. He felt obligated to marry her because he'd been responsible for taking her virginity—even though she'd slept with him because she wanted to. And as much as she might want to hand all the blame to Griff and Dawson for this marriage, she couldn't. If she hadn't felt there was a small chance for happiness, she would have faced her family, confessed what she'd done, and taken her lumps. She married Dawson with every hope that they could make this relationship work.

But the truth was, Dawson didn't want her.

He ran a hand through his hair. "Look, Mattie, we both know this isn't a real marriage. You agreed under duress, and I want you to know that I don't expect…anything."

Mattie was tired, more so than she'd ever been in her life. And every fiber of her being was focused on one thing: not letting the tears burning the backs of her eyes fall. She didn't have the energy to figure out how she felt about this. She was too tired to argue. She was too tired to be angry. Unfortunately, there was one emotion she wasn't too tired to feel. Profound sadness.

"I'll take the master bedroom," she said. She wasn't too tired to want this to be as difficult, annoying and inconvenient for him as possible. He might put her in another room, but he wouldn't be able to ignore her presence.

"Okay. I'll put your suitcases in there." He picked

them up. "Do you mind if I move my stuff out in the morning?"

"Not at all," she said.

She didn't care if he moved it or left it. She didn't care about much at that moment—except that he not see how very much he had hurt her.

Dawson cut through the water in the pool, kicking and stroking his way from one end to the other. He added more laps. The swim had felt good. He'd needed the exercise. Translation: He wanted Mattie more than he'd wanted any woman—ever. He'd never experienced a more hellish night. A night spent tossing, turning and thinking about Mattie. And he'd awakened in an acute state of need. The cold water and the cold late-November air, he'd hoped, would take the edge off his tension.

But he was still strung tighter than a brand-new fiddle. He couldn't get the expression on her face out of his mind. She'd looked like a kid who'd just been told there was no Santa Claus, Tooth Fairy, or Easter Bunny—all at the same time. She was crushed. It was as if all the animation, energy and joy had gone out of her.

And he was responsible.

He knew in his gut, though, that keeping her at arm's length was the right thing. Although he wanted her in his bed almost more than he wanted his next breath, separate rooms was his punishment to bear for taking advantage of her naiveté. It would never happen again. He'd sunk to his father's level. The first chance he'd gotten, he'd used her innocence and seduced her.

He'd made one mistake, but he wouldn't compound it by turning his back on her *or* renewing their intimate relationship. He wasn't worthy of her love. And using her that way would only hurt her more in the long run. Someday she would understand that he'd done this for her.

His muscles ached from the exertion of his swim, and he hauled himself out of the pool and picked up a towel.

"She'll thank me for keeping the distance between us," he mumbled to himself as he dried off. "Yeah, when pigs fly." He laughed, a bitter, hollow sound, as he slung the towel across his shoulders.

"How long are you gonna stand there talking to yourself?"

He whirled around and looked up at Mattie, bent over and resting her elbows on the balcony outside the kitchen.

"You're up early," he said, grinning in spite of himself at the saucy picture she made. Oversize T-shirt that said Dallas Cowboys on the front. Black sweatpants slightly pulled up to reveal slender ankles and bare feet. Barefoot and pregnant. The thought made his blood run cold. Naw. Couldn't happen. It had only been one time. He took a deep breath.

"I always get up at the crack of dawn," she said. "Do you want some breakfast?" She angled her head toward the room behind her. "I've got bacon, eggs, pancakes, hash browns."

"I didn't know you could cook."

"You still don't know that I can. I could be lying about the food. I could be telling the truth about the cooking part, but consuming it might take the constitution of a garbage truck. Why don't you come on up here and see for yourself whether or not I'm telling the truth."

"All right, you're on. Give me a couple of minutes to shower. And I'll be right up."

"The clock is ticking." She turned around and went back inside.

Anticipation hummed through him as he quickly showered and dried off. He put on sweats and a T-shirt, the only clothes he'd brought downstairs last night. He would need to dress for work soon. He'd been neglecting things at the office.

When he walked into the kitchen, the delicious smells made his mouth water. Almost as much as did the sight of Mattie—blond hair tucked behind her ears, cheeks pink from her culinary exertions, gray eyes shining as she stood by the stove watching the bubbles on her pancakes pop.

She flipped them over. "I hope you're hungry."

"Starved," he said, his gaze lowering to her long legs.

"The table is set. Take a seat, and I'll bring everything over when these are done."

He noticed the drip coffeemaker waited with a full, fresh pot. "Would you like some coffee?" he asked.

"I don't drink it," she said, glancing over her shoulder at him. "I just figured since you had the contraption, you probably did. I found the can of coffee in the fridge and made a pot."

"It smells great."

And so do you, he thought as they stood shoulder to shoulder. She flipped flapjacks, while he poured himself coffee. Domestic as hell.

And he realized he liked it.

He thought back, and realized that no woman had ever made him breakfast before. At least not in his house. No woman had stayed overnight before. It was his rule, because he never wanted a woman to feel used. Now he had a wife. She had made him breakfast. Inside, he was grinning like the fool he no doubt was.

"Sit down," she said again. "Everything is ready."

He took his seat across from the slider that looked out on the balcony. The table was set for two, with the green, woven placemats and matching cloth napkins that Mallory had sent him for a housewarming gift. Juice was poured and the center of the table was filled with jars and bottles that contained syrup, butter, ketchup, Tabasco, salsa.

Mattie brought him a plate piled with hash browns, bacon, eggs, pancakes and wheat toast. Ruefully she inspected the lack of room on the table as she set the food in front of him.

"I found all this in the refrigerator, but I didn't know what you liked. So I put it all out."

Sort of like she did with everything. Put it out there, and what you see is what you get. He admired that about her. No pretense. No games. Pure honesty.

"Thanks, Mattie. It looks great. Smells even better."

"This is the moment of truth," she said, filling a plate for herself. She sat down at a right angle to him. "Now you get to judge whether or not I'm a good cook."

He found he was hungry. After putting butter and syrup on the flapjacks, he tasted a bite. It melted in his mouth. He sampled some of everything and said, "This tastes good."

She smiled. "I'm glad."

They ate in silence for a few moments. Finally Dawson said, "Where did you learn to cook like this?"

"My mother." She ate a forkful of eggs. "With all of us kids and Dad to feed, she always needed a hand in the kitchen. I picked it up by osmosis, I guess."

"I figured you were always out in the north forty with the horses."

She shrugged. "I did that, too."

He realized that they hadn't had an opportunity to discuss what she would do after they got married.

"Horses have always been a big part of your life?" he asked.

She nodded as she nibbled on a piece of toast. "For as far back as I can remember. I can't imagine not training horses."

"You live a long way from the ranch now."

"Not that far. I worked it out before the wedding yesterday."

"You did?"

She nodded. "Ethan offered to pick me up. Uncle Ryan said I could use one of the ranch vehicles until we make other arrangements."

Cowboys. The thought tightened his gut like wet rawhide drying in the sun. His wife alone with a cowboy. He didn't like the idea of that. Not one single bit.

"I'll drive you to the ranch," he said.

She stopped nibbling and stared at him. "I have it worked out. It's not your problem."

"It's no trouble."

She glanced at the clock on the stove and jumped up. "Can we talk about this tonight?"

Tonight. The word conjured an image of twisted sheets with Mattie lying in the middle of them. Her hair tangled from his hands. Her mouth swollen from his kisses. Her body satisfied from his loving. Instantly he was hard and ready. If he was going to keep his distance from her, that was a bad sign.

"I'm not sure what time I'll be home," he said.

The light in her eyes, so bright only moments before, seemed to flicker and go out. "I've got to change. Ethan will be here any minute." She hurried from the room.

He stared for a long time at her half-eaten food. "Someday you'll thank me, Mattie."

As she'd walked down the aisle to him, he'd seen through her bluster to the tender heart beneath. He'd promised to keep her from hurt, even if he was the potential source of that hurt.

Twelve

Mattie mulled over the events of the last week. They'd settled into a daily routine, except for Thanksgiving Day. Ryan and Lily had invited them to the big family gathering on the ranch. She and Dawson had played newlyweds to the hilt. But as she put the finishing touches on the latest chicken recipe she was trying, she shook her head. She knew she was no closer to getting Dawson into her bed—or rather into his bed with her—than she'd been seven days ago. She'd played Hannah Homemaker long enough and was darn well ready for some payback.

"Gotta rattle his cage," she said to herself. "And I think I know just how to do it."

That morning she'd asked if there was any way she could have the car. They hadn't discussed getting another vehicle and the ranch truck she'd been using needed an overhaul. He'd arranged to ride to the office with his friend Zane. He and his wife Gwen also had a house in Kingston Estates, not far from Dawson's.

Mattie had done her wifely errands: a stop at the cleaner's to drop off his suits, at the grocery store. So much for the way to a man's heart being through his stomach. Apparently she needed to find the detour to Dawson's ticker. All week she'd been cooking semi-gourmet meals, but although he had nothing but praise for the results, he hadn't invited himself back into his own bed beside her.

She knew if their marriage stood a ghost of a chance for success, that had to happen. She'd also thought about doing the inviting, but was afraid her fragile ego couldn't handle a rejection. So on to Plan B: a *romantic* dinner.

Her purchases had included a bouquet of flowers for the table, along with scented candles. And a new outfit. That part had taken the longest. She'd found her way into Dawson's arms the first time with the help of a dynamite dress. This outfit had to be just right. Subtle, but sexy. Attention-getting, but seductive. Figure-flattering, but not too obvious.

She glanced at the sliding glass doors that acted as a mirror against the dark night outside. She'd chosen a white lounging outfit from a well-known lingerie store. The pants tied at the waist, were loose at the hip, but tapered to a crew band at the ankle. The matching short top had a scooped neckline to accentuate her breasts and show just a hint of cleavage, yet it skimmed her waist, flashing her midriff when she moved a certain way.

"I hope this does the trick," she said to herself.

She walked into the family room and surveyed the small table she'd set up in front of the fireplace. "Tablecloth, check. Flowers, check. Crystal wineglasses, check."

She took a long wooden match from the slender box beside the hearth and lit the gas fireplace. A cheerful blaze instantly ignited.

In the kitchen, she sprinkled cheese on the chicken dish, the final touch before sticking it in the oven. The question was how long to bake it. She glanced at the clock and noted that it was five-thirty. Dawson had been walking in the door from work earlier and earlier every day. She hadn't a clue how to judge cooking time to coordinate with his arrival. She put the dish in the oven and hoped for the best. She'd done everything humanly possible to create a romantic atmosphere. There was nothing more she could do, short of greeting her husband at the door wearing nothing but a smile.

The thought made her chuckle. She could probably manage the nerve to do that, but hoped it wouldn't be necessary. It would be so much more satisfying if Dawson undressed her. The thought sent shivers over her flesh.

An outside sound drifted to her, like a car door closing. She was still adjusting to the different noises of a new house in the suburbs, and wasn't certain. Then she heard the front door open and close.

"Dawson?"

"Yeah." He walked into the kitchen.

Mattie looked at him, white shirt with sleeves rolled up to the elbow, tie at half-staff, suit coat slung over his arm, briefcase in hand. Her insides quivered and the blood raced through her veins. Who'd have guessed that a rumpled executive instead of a Texas cowboy would tug at her heart this way?

She moved around the center island work area to where he stood on the other side. His eyes darkened, and he started to lean toward her. A hi-honey-I'm-home kiss? Lord, she hoped so. She would make it a welcome-back-at-the-end-of-a-long-day kiss that he wouldn't forget in a hurry.

But he seemed to catch himself, and he straightened. He turned away and set his briefcase down.

"How was your day?" she asked. Isn't that what a wife said when her husband arrived home after work? Even if she didn't get a kiss? Sheer force of will kept her voice cheerful and her disappointment at bay.

He nodded. "Good. Profits are up in all areas of the business. We're considering an expansion in the real estate market. All in all, I'd say things are going well." Sniffing, he said, "I don't smell anything cooking."

That was a good sign, wasn't it? The fact that he expected food when he arrived home from work?

"You should soon. I just put dinner in the oven. I wasn't sure when you'd be home."

"I guess I should have called." He looked at the empty kitchen table. "I'll put out plates and utensils, if you want."

"I've already done it."

"I guess we're using the invisible china and flatware tonight?" He raised one eyebrow questioningly.

She laughed. "No. It's in the family room."

He turned to look, and she saw his shoulders tense when he spotted the candle-and-flower-bedecked table in front of the fireplace and the brightly burning blaze.

"Oh, I forgot something," she said.

"You could have fooled me," he answered, an edge to his voice.

She walked over to one of the cupboards and opened it, looking up for what she wanted. She could have sworn there was an ice bucket in there. She planned to keep the wine bottle chilled on the table. On the top shelf, she spotted what she was looking for, and lifted her arms in an attempt to get it down.

"Let me do that," Dawson said, his tone annoyed, and just this side of abrasive.

"I can get it," she said, reaching higher. She felt the hem of her top brush the undersides of her breasts.

"Don't," he said. He moved behind her and put his hands on her arms, lowering them to her sides. Then he gently but firmly moved her aside. "You'll strain yourself. I'll get it."

He easily lifted down the ice bucket.

"Thanks," she said, then pulled a bottle of wine from the refrigerator. "Would you like to do the honors?"

He shook his head and a muscle tightened in his jaw. "Actually, I just remembered that there's some work at the office I need to finish." His voice sounded strangled. "Zane was in a hurry to get home to Gwen, and I completely forgot about some figures—" his gaze lowered to her midriff, then went lower to her ankles "—I mean numbers. I have some numbers to work up. Very important," he mumbled as he picked up his briefcase and headed to the lower level of the house where the garage was located. "I just came home for the car. Don't hold dinner. I'm not sure how long this is going to take."

She heard him exit the house, then the car door slam. The automatic garage door went up, then down again after he backed out. Then she heard the sound of a car leaving the drive.

Mattie pulled her casserole from the oven and disgustedly tossed the pot holders on the ceramic tile countertop. "You're not the only chicken who lives here," she said, hearing the catch in her voice.

Feeling like a rejected sixteen-year-old again, Mattie walked over to her romantic table and turned over Dawson's plate. "It takes a special kind of stupid to turn down what I'm offering,'' she said to the empty room.

Then she brushed the single tear from her cheek as she turned off the fire in the hearth. If only the fire inside her could be snuffed out as easily.

"So you want to tell me what happened?" Mallory Prescott Fortune asked.

Standing beside his sister on the balcony outside his kitchen, Dawson studied her. He sometimes forgot how beautiful she was. Only three inches shorter than his own five foot eleven, she was tall and slender. Her hazel eyes were the same shade as his own, as was her long brown sun-streaked hair. She and her new husband Reed had joined he and Mattie for a goodbye dinner before heading back to Australia. Reed planned to modernize his family's horse operation patterning it after techniques he'd been observing on the Double Crown Ranch. Mallory wanted to use her degree in interior design. While he talked to his sister, Mattie and Reed were in the family room sharing horse stories.

"What happened?" he said, repeating her question. "Nothing happened."

That was a bald-faced lie. Since he didn't know how long it would be before he saw his sister again, he didn't want to spoil this visit with anything as disturbing as the truth. Because the truth was that *everything* had happened—all of it bad. His whole life had turned upside down, and he deserved every moment of hell he was going through.

Hellish experience number 1—putting Mattie in a separate bedroom when he wanted her so much that he ached from it. Hellish experience number 2—sharing a wonderful breakfast with her, only to learn that she was going to spend the day with the cowboys on the Double Crown. Jealousy had licked at him until she'd met him at the door that night. She'd made a great dinner and had done the same every night since...setting him up for hellish experience number 3—having to save her from him by turning his back on the romantic evening she'd created. Every nerve in his body had urged him to scoop her into his arms, carry her off to bed and make love to her all night long.

He wasn't sure how long he could share living space with her before making love to her again. If he didn't care about her so much, it wouldn't be a problem. But the last thing he wanted was to hurt her any more than he already had.

"Sell it to someone who's buying, Dawson." Mallory shook her head in disgust. "This is me you're talking to. Something happened all right. Your wedding to Mattie had all the earmarks of a shotgun wedding. I could practically see the imprint of a double-barrel on the back of your tux. How did you and Mattie wind up married?"

He sighed. "Have you ever analyzed the power of guilt?"

"No. But I think I see where you're headed. Do you want to tell it like it is, or should I just use my overactive imagination?"

"I seduced Mattie. She was a virgin. If that isn't bad enough, her brother Griff found us."

"Oh, Lord." Mallory shook her head sympathetically. Then she made a great show of checking him over from head to toe. "No broken bones. I don't recall any black eyes or bruises to spoil the wedding photos. How did Griff convince you to marry Mattie?" She snapped her fingers. "Shotgun."

He laughed. "If he has one, I never saw it." Dawson rested his elbows on the railing and looked out over the pool, the cement deck and the grass area beyond. "He brought the subject up, but not before I'd come to the same conclusion. Marrying her was the only thing to do. It's my fault that we're in this mess."

"First of all, I think you need to cut yourself some slack on the seduction issue. Mattie is a tomboy with the heart of a temptress."

"What's that supposed to mean?" he asked, not sure whether or not he needed to defend his wife's honor. But the vision of candles, flowers, fireplace and Mattie in an outfit that left him hard and aching flashed through his mind. Definitely a temptress.

"She grew up with five brothers on a ranch. Then she gets a haircut and a makeup lesson, and turns into a raving beauty ready to take that new look out for a spin and see what it can do. What it did was speed up your libido from zero to sixty in the blink of an eye. Bottom line, Dawson—it takes two to tango."

"That's a cliché."

"Because it's true. You are not the only one to blame for this."

"That's what Mattie said as she turned down my first two marriage proposals."

Mallory smiled as she nodded approvingly. "I knew I liked her. How did you get her to accept?"

"Actually, Griff did, by invoking the words that strike terror into any kid's heart—what will Mom and Dad say? But if I'd had more self-control, we wouldn't be in this situation."

"Mattie Fortune—Prescott," she amended, "doesn't strike me as the kind of woman who can be forced to do something she doesn't want to do. Case in point, her wedding ensemble."

Dawson grinned. "She was really something, wasn't she?"

"Yes, and like I said, she has the heart of a temptress. I'd lay odds that her heart is set on you."

"That's where you're wrong," Dawson scoffed. "What would she see in me? I'm just like Dad."

"That makes you a Prescott," Mallory said with a smile. "And you have all of the best Prescott qualities."

"You're biased," he said, returning her smile.

"True. But that's not the point," his sister answered.

"Then what is?"

"You only get one shot at the great love of your life. I think Mattie is yours."

"And why's that?" he asked.

"Because no one can force us Prescotts to do anything we don't want to do. For example, I ran out on my wedding to the man my parents chose because I knew in my heart he wasn't 'the one.' When I met Reed, sparks flew. The same thing happened to you when you met Mattie."

He laughed. "We wanted to strangle each other."

"So did Reed and I. But he was the right one. In a nutshell—don't blow it, bro. You'll regret it."

When she finished her heartfelt speech, Dawson leaned down and kissed her cheek.

"What was that for?" she asked.

"For being such a romantic."

"And smart, too," she said, giving him a hug. "Think about it."

"Will do."

Later, her brother and Reed went to the market while Mattie sat on the couch in the family room, staring thoughtfully into the blazing fire. Her sister-in-law sat cross-legged on the floor beside the hearth, clearly savoring the warmth.

"What's wrong, Mattie?" she asked.

"I forgot about dessert."

"No worries," Mallory said.

"Are you making fun of my accent or do you just like that expression?" Mattie asked with a fleeting grin.

"Both. But truly, don't worry about it. Dawson and Reed will be back in a few minutes with something to satisfy our sweet tooth. I'm sending mental telepathy that it's to be gooey and chocolate."

"I feel so inadequate. What kind of a wife am I?" She bit the corner of her lip, cutting off the threat of a sob slipping out. Her anxiety had nothing to do with chocolate, and everything to do with the fact that she couldn't make Dawson invite her into his bed.

"What is it?" Mallory asked. "This is more than just forgetting dessert. Is it the circumstances of your marriage?"

"You know about that?" Mattie felt her cheeks grow warm, and it certainly wasn't from the fire in the fireplace. Reluctantly, she met her sister-in-law's gaze.

"Dawson told me pretty much everything. He said you tried to take the blame, too, but Griff wouldn't listen."

"My brother is a blockhead. And for a brilliant man, *your* brother is a moron." Mattie realized what she'd said and who she'd said it to. "I'm sorry, Mallory. I didn't mean—"

"Yes, you did," she interrupted. "And when you're right, far be it from me to contradict you. But why do *you* think he's a moron?"

Mattie threw up her hands. "I've tried everything I can think of to make this marriage work."

"Why isn't it working? It's only been a short time. How can you tell?"

"For starters, we aren't sleeping in the same bed. I bet Brody and Jillian don't have that problem. Or you and Reed." Mattie saw the dreamy smile on her sister-in-law's face, and knew she'd spent last night in the arms of the man she loved.

"No, we definitely sleep in the same bed," Mallory said, confirming her suspicions. "But you two are newlyweds. You've already done the wild thing. I don't understand why you—"

"I don't want things to be this way," she assured the other woman. "But I'm afraid to just come out and ask him about it. If he turned me down, I don't know if I could take it—" She bit her lip again.

"Have you tried?"

"Seducing him?" Mattie nodded vigorously. "I fixed a wonderful dinner, set out candles and flowers in front of the fireplace. Got a bottle of wine. Bought a sensational outfit."

"What happened?" Mallory asked.

"He mumbled something about having unfinished work at the office. He couldn't get out of here fast enough. He just doesn't want me."

"I don't believe that for a second. If anything, my guess would be that he's trying to protect you."

"From what?" Mattie asked, bewildered.

"I couldn't say. But Dawson takes care of the people he loves. He married you to protect you. And tonight I've seen the way he looks at you whenever you're in the room. He can't take his eyes off you. Mattie, he's a goner."

"You're just a hopeless romantic," Mattie scoffed. "I don't think I believe in happy endings anymore."

"I'm a hope*ful* romantic. Although I admit your happy ending might take a bit of work." Mallory shifted her position, stretching her legs out as if they were cramped.

"What kind of work?"

"Make him jealous," her sister-in-law suggested. "It worked for me with your brother. When my ex-fiancé showed up here, it got Reed's attention in a big way."

"But I don't have an ex-fiancé. I've never even had another boyfriend. How am I going to make Dawson jealous?"

"You work at the Double Crown, right?"

Mattie nodded. "But the cowboys are my friends. Almost like brothers to me."

"Dawson doesn't know that."

"I have to admit, he didn't seem too happy when I told him one of the cowboys was picking me up and giving me a ride to the ranch," she admitted.

"See?" Mallory said, warming to her subject.

"I don't know," Mattie said, shaking her head doubtfully. "I don't think I can play games like that."

"If my brother is as jealous as I think he is, you won't have to do anything but stand next to another guy."

"I'll think about it," Mattie agreed. "Thanks for listening."

The front door opened and her brother Reed walked in with Dawson right behind him. Mattie's heart beat faster at the sight of her husband. Was Mallory right? Would she get his attention if he thought another man was interested in her?

Reed went directly to his wife and kissed her. Mattie sighed at the appealing picture they made. Her brother's blond hair, pale blue eyes, and rugged good looks were an attractive counterpoint to his wife's femininity.

Dawson set a package on the kitchen table, then joined them in the family room. "So what have you girls been talking about?" he asked, looking from one to the other.

Mallory's eyes took on a mischievous twinkle as she said, "Not much. Just about brothers being block-heads."

Thirteen

Two weeks later, Dawson decided his sister's words definitely fit him to a *T* tonight. He was, indeed, a blockhead.

He'd left the warmth of his house in the suburbs. His suit jacket was forgotten in the car. And now he hunched his shoulders against the bitter December wind as he walked to the barn on the Double Crown. After work, he'd driven to the ranch, poked his head in the house to say a quick hello to Ryan and Lily, then headed back out into the cold. Why?

Mattie.

The answer came to him as clear as the Texas sky above filled with twinkling stars. When she'd called the office and left a message with his secretary that she would be home late, he'd decided to drop by and surprise her. But on the drive out, he'd realized a couple of things.

His reasoning had less to do with a surprise, than it did with the fact that he didn't relish the idea of going home to an empty house. Somehow, Mattie had insinuated herself into his life, and she'd done it without effort in a sinfully short period of time. That big, cold house without her warm, whirlwind presence was as desolate as the Texas prairie on a cloudy night.

The second reason he'd driven out here had a whole lot to do with atonement. Ever since the night he'd run out on her romantic dinner, he'd been haunted by the wounded look in her gray eyes. He hadn't meant to hurt her. In fact, every single thing he did was to keep from doing just that.

"And it's working just great," he muttered sarcastically. The wind howled past his ears in response.

She was young and vulnerable; he was older and wiser. It was up to him to take charge and make sure she didn't get in over her head with a guy like him. If he were a better man, a man worthy of love from a woman like Mattie, things would be different. But he'd proved in spades that he wasn't. All he could do now was minimize battle damage and protect her from himself.

The third reason he'd decided to surprise her was to protect Mattie from other guys who had things on their minds besides transportation to and from the ranch. No way could he convince her not to work on the Double Crown. The horses were too important to her. And she was too good with them. She had a gift, and it would be a crime if she didn't use it. But the thought of the Double Crown ranch hands using their hands on her while chauffeuring her made him nuts. Until he got her a car of her own, he decided, he would taxi her back and forth himself.

He stopped outside the barn and saw light around the door, then heard voices. When he recognized Mattie's, his breath quickened. It had nothing to do with walking uphill; it was the seductive quality wrapped around every word that passed her full, kissable lips that made him hard with need. Next he heard a masculine voice, and his gut clenched. It hadn't occurred to him that she was working with anyone else. Who was in there with her?

The door creaked as he swung it wide, and instantly the scents that assailed him left no doubt that he was in a barn. He looked down the dusty, hay-strewn aisle between gated stalls, spotting Mattie at the end—with a guy he'd never seen before. A cowboy. A *young* cowboy. No doubt about that, what with the hat, boots, denims and work shirt. At this distance he couldn't tell for sure, but he thought the cowboy was just a kid, closer to Mattie's age than his own. The thought made his throat constrict.

He watched her for a moment, coiling a length of rope. Her movements were graceful and confident. She was in her element, her world. When she reached up to hang the lariat on the nail nearby, Dawson's gut tightened another notch. A vision flashed through his mind of her midriff, her flesh bared to his gaze as her top slid up bit by bit, when she stretched for something in his kitchen cupboard. The memory made him long to see even a glimpse of her beautiful breasts. If he'd stayed a second longer that evening, he would have stretched her out on the kitchen table and made love to her right there. Had she known what the sight of her that way did to him? Was she trying to make the young cowboy feel that same gut-twisting need? Like he wanted to scoop her up, lay her out, and love her until neither of them had any strength left? At the thought of another man touching her that way, white-hot fury shot through him.

When she'd replaced the rope, Mattie leaned back against the gate, one leg bent with her boot heel resting on a slat. The cowboy stood across from her, thumbs hooked in his jeans pockets. Neither of them had noticed him yet. If she'd been with anyone besides a cowboy, his blood pressure might have stayed steady.

But he knew that kid was exactly the kind of mate she'd wanted for herself, and Dawson had robbed her of the chance to be with him.

The thought made him angry—mostly at himself. Even though he knew it was wrong, it added insult to injury. All he could think about was getting her away from this guy and having her all to himself.

He started toward them, and his shoes rustled the straw.

She looked up, straightening as he drew closer. "Dawson."

"Mattie."

"You're probably the last person I would have expected to see in the barn," she said, glancing at his dusty black loafers and city-slicker slacks.

Was that a guilty look on her face? He was a couple of feet away and couldn't tell for sure. It could have been pleasure at the sight of him, but he wouldn't bet his last dollar on it. Why would she be glad to see him? She was with a good-looking cowboy. A *young*, good-looking cowboy. Dawson suddenly felt old and tired. Old and just plain old. Followed by more old and really angry. A combustible combination.

"I got your message, that you were working late," he said.

She nodded. "The foreman hired a new hand."

"Yeah. So I noticed." He eyed kid cowboy.

Mattie glanced at her lanky, dark-haired, blue-eyed companion. "This is Zach Conroy. All the other guys had errands in town. I offered to show him the ropes."

"Literally?" Dawson asked, glancing at the rope she had just hung up.

She chuckled. "No pun intended."

Zach stuck his hand out. "Nice to meet you, sir."

Dawson winced at the word *sir,* a term of respect he'd always given his father. Since Dawson had turned into a Geoffrey Prescott clone, he figured "sir" was probably appropriate. But having the word directed at him was like having salt rubbed in a festering wound.

He contemplated ignoring the kid's hand, but couldn't forget that he was also his mother's son, taught to mind his manners. "Welcome to the Double Crown, Zach. You couldn't have a better teacher than my *wife.*"

"No, sir." The kid slid him a nervous look.

"My *husband* is a shameless flatterer." Mattie mimicked his emphasis, but she looked at him as if he'd grown another head.

"It's not flattery if it's the truth," he countered.

"Dawson, what are you doing all the way out here?" she asked, her tone reflecting confusion that was just this side of exasperation.

Protecting you from the likes of him, he thought. Instead he said, "I'm here to give you a lift home."

She smiled warmly as if his explanation pleased her. "What a nice surprise. Shall I ask Aunt Lily if we can stay for supper. It's late and—"

He shot Zach a withering glance, then took her arm and started walking toward the door. "Mattie's off duty. You're on your own, kid," he said to the cowboy. In a lower voice he said to her, "It is late. I want to get you home."

Get you home.

The words sang through Mattie's mind all the way to the house. They were just dripping with suggestion. What would he do with her when he got her home? She dearly hoped that it would be more than when he'd gotten her home on their wedding night. She fervently prayed it would be a lot more than her dismal failure of a romantic dinner. Maybe his feelings were changing. He certainly hadn't acted like himself when he'd found her in the barn with Zach.

Was he jealous? Was Mallory right about his showing his affection if he thought she was interested in someone else? There was unmistakable strain in him. He'd hardly said two words all the way home. He'd driven as if he couldn't leave the ranch behind fast enough. And his pace never slowed as they set a land-speed record on the highway back to the house. Her body hummed with anticipation, and her heart soared with hope that he would love her, body and soul.

He braked the car in front of the garage and pressed the door opener. Mattie opened her mouth to say something, then glanced at Dawson. Tension hardened his features and tightened his mouth to a straight line. His shoulders were rigid and his knuckles white as he gripped the steering wheel.

She closed her mouth. It could wait.

They entered the kitchen, and Mattie suddenly felt grungy from her day's work. "I'm going to take a shower," she said.

"Suit yourself."

Not the response of a man intent on ravishing his woman, she thought as doubt crept in. She went into her room and stripped off her boots, jeans, shirt and undergarments. In the shower, she washed her hair as she puzzled over Dawson. He was annoyed with her, and she wasn't exactly sure why. It had something to do with Zach. But Zach was just a kid. The more she puzzled, the more uneasy she became. Her neck muscles tightened and she realized Dawson's tension was contagious. Damn him, anyway. She always looked forward to her evening shower. Thanks to him and his little tizzy, she couldn't even enjoy it. Maybe it was time to get things out in the open between them.

She shut the water off, then grabbed a big, fluffy bath towel and wrapped it around herself. In her dressing area, she took another towel and dried her hair, before running a comb through it. When she walked into her bedroom, she saw Dawson standing beside the bed. She had the feeling that he'd paced like a caged beast while she'd showered. His eyes had the look of a hungry tiger ready to do battle for his primal needs. She clutched her towel, then realized she wasn't exactly dressed for battle. Or was she?

"If you're through, I have a few things to say to you." He planted his feet wide apart. Then, almost unwillingly, his gaze lowered from her eyes to the knot where her towel came together over her breasts. His eyes narrowed and his nostrils flared slightly as if he were scenting his prey. "Put some clothes on first."

"Just say what you have to say." She might not have her armor on, but she wasn't going to back down from a confrontation. She lowered her hands to her sides and lifted her chin. "Fire when ready," she said.

"Your call," he said with a shrug. But his hands were a little unsteady as he stuck them in his pockets. "For starters—you and Zach alone in the barn."

Aha! She'd been right. At least he didn't beat around the bush. "I already told you. I offered to show him the ranch. In your line of work I believe you call it 'orientation.'"

"And just what else were you *orienting* him about?" he asked, his eyes narrowing on her. "The two of you looked mighty cozy."

"I resent your tone and that question. We were merely talking."

"I didn't like it."

"He's new. He doesn't know anyone. We were just getting acquainted."

"I still didn't like it."

"Why not? What in the world was there to object to? Talking in the barn?"

"Maybe the fact that nine out of ten guys talking to a beautiful woman in the barn would want a roll in the hay."

Her temper snapped. "Apparently I married number ten, the only man who doesn't want me—in the barn, in his bed, or anywhere else for that matter."

"Shows how much you know about men," he muttered. His gaze raked over her—from her bare feet and legs, over her abdomen, to her breasts. A muscle in his jaw contracted, and his eyes darkened. "Where's your common sense, Mattie? You don't know that guy."

"No. But all my instincts tell me he's a good guy."

"You're a sitting duck all alone in the barn. What if your instincts were wrong?"

She hoped to God they were right, because her instincts were commanding her to do something now, that could send her to heaven—or land her in hell. She was going to put everything on the line—her body, her heart, her soul.

Mattie dropped her towel. "My mother once said that arguing naked was the prescription for a healthy marriage." But she was so scared that he would turn his back on her. Then what would she do?

He swallowed hard as his eyes devoured her. "Only

one of us is naked,'' he said in a hoarse voice, as one corner of his mouth quirked.

At least he'd stopped yelling at her about being alone in the barn. But that wasn't all. The bulge in his slacks told her that he wanted her.

Mattie's heart started to pound when he moved toward her. He reached out a trembling hand and cupped her face in his palm. It was the only sign she needed. She started to unbutton his shirt. He ripped it from his waistband, then helped her with the buttons before dragging it off his shoulders. Her breath caught at the sight of his bare chest, its masculine sprinkling of hair tapering down to disappear into his trousers.

As if he knew what she was thinking, he unbuckled his belt and undid the hook on his pants. The bulge there made her heart and spirit soar with the knowledge of her power.

Then he met her gaze. She knew he was giving her the opportunity to refuse to go any further. This was the point of no return.

She reached out and rested her hand over his heart, and felt it pound. ''One of us still has too many clothes on,'' she said, her tone husky.

He sucked in a breath. ''I'm luckier than nine out of ten guys. And you're mistaken about me not wanting you.''

''I've never been happier to be wrong,'' she whispered, her heart so full that she didn't trust her voice.

His eyes darkened even more, and in the next instant Dawson gripped her arms just short of hurting her. He lowered his mouth to hers in a crushing kiss. Her heart beat so hard that it nearly flew from her chest as her breathing escalated. In spite of his words, she felt the anger and passion warring within him. She had no idea what demons he struggled against. But for now, it was just her and Dawson and if there was any justice in the world, she would make him forget everything but her.

Mattie opened her mouth to him, inviting him inside. When his tongue invaded, she touched it with the tip of her own, and smiled with satisfaction when his breathing grew more ragged. She felt his desperation, his urgency, as he backed away long enough to tear off the rest of his clothes. Then she was in his arms, skin to skin, soft to hard, woman to man.

He backed her up until she felt the bed behind her. The next thing she knew, she was on her back with Dawson above her. He spread her legs apart with his knee, and she willingly obliged. With a gentleness that belied the fierce expression on his face, he touched her most intimate femininity. As he inserted a finger, she felt herself throbbing; she closed around him, welcoming this imitation of the intimacy she craved.

"You're so ready," he said in a strangled voice.

Shocked at her boldness, yet trusting her instincts, she took his manhood in her hand. He sucked in a breath and trembled. "So are you," she murmured.

She stroked his shaft and marveled at the silky softness. Moving her hand slowly, tenderly, she explored him.

He gasped and put his hand over hers. "Stop."

"Why?"

"If you don't, in about ten seconds it will be all over." He closed his eyes and shuddered. There was a fierce look of concentration on his face. When he opened his eyes, he said, "Besides, I don't want to hurt you."

"How can this hurt me? You don't need to protect

me. Not from this. I want you. I've wanted you ever since that first time. Don't you get it? Just love me—''

"Damn it, Mattie.'' His voice was nearly a growl. "You don't know what you're saying.''

"Yes, I do. You can roar at me all you want. But I am woman—I'll roar right back.''

Despite his words, he continued to stroke her. As bolts of desire zapped her, she found it increasingly difficult to think straight. To make a rational argument about why it was all right to continue doing what they were doing. It was time to just do it. Still holding him in her hand, she positioned him at the opening of her womanhood. She smiled to herself when he groaned.

"I have to be inside you.''

"Yes. Please. Now,'' she cried.

He entered her fast and hard, and she gloried in his possession. She had never felt more feminine, more womanly than she did at this moment. There was no pain this time, just pure physical satisfaction and intense pleasure that flowed through her like liquid fire. Oh, she was warm. Every part of her was hot.

He leaned forward to kiss her, and at the same time took most of his weight on his elbows. She lifted her hips, thrusting against him.

"Easy, Mattie. Slow and easy does it.'' Dawson brushed the hair back from her face and gently kissed her forehead, nose, jaw, and a spot just beneath her ear that nearly sent her to the great beyond. "I've wanted you, too, ever since the first time. I'm not sure I can hold out.''

"We've got all night,'' she said, frustrated. She'd waited, too, and she was *ready*.

"Yes.'' But he continued to kiss her face slowly, sweetly.

She throbbed with need and started a slow, subtle, sexy hip rhythm. "Please, Dawson."

He groaned again. "Mattie, stop."

"Please, Dawson," she said, sensing his imminent surrender.

"Not yet."

She wiggled against him and heard his sharp intake of breath. "Witch," he growled. "If that's the way you want it."

"It is," she answered.

"You asked for it."

He moved against her, and she received him as he thrust again and again. In the center of her belly, a knot tightened. With each lunge she felt herself moving closer and closer to the breaking point. She wrapped her legs around him, and this time his rasping breath seemed to come from deep in his soul.

"Oh, Mattie. That feels so good."

"I'm glad," she whispered, placing her palms on his chest. She brushed the pads of her thumbs across his nipples and felt them tighten.

With every thrust, the pressure inside her built, until she silently begged for release. Finally, there was a jolt of electricity where their bodies joined that created an explosion of bright light behind her eyes. Tremors shook her body. His arms shaking with tension, Dawson held her until she went still. Then he lunged once more and stopped. Her eyes opened in time to see a fierce look on his face. He made a sound deep in his throat, then he gathered her to his chest as he claimed his own release.

He rolled to his side. Still holding her in his arms, he carried her with him and snuggled her against him.

His chest expanded from the huge breath he took in. ''So,'' he said.

''So,'' she answered.

''How do you feel?''

Good question. Warm fuzzys. Glowing. Content. Happy. The feelings were so big, so deep, so wonderful, she didn't have the words to express the delicious sensation. So she simply said, ''I love you.''

Fourteen

Dawson straightened his tie as he walked down the hall to the kitchen. The smells of breakfast drifted to him and his mouth started to water, not so much at the thought of food, but at the thought of the cook. *Mattie.* How had she so quickly become part of his life?

Waking up with her in his arms just a short time ago was the best thing that had ever happened to him. Her silky hair had spilled over his shoulders and trickled down his chest, teasing him with erotic promise. He had never seen a more beautiful sight than a drowsy Mattie, blinking sleep from her eyes, then her radiant smile when she'd noticed that he was watching her. Followed again by the words that still shook him to his soul.

I love you.

The happiness in her expression slipped a little when he hadn't responded in kind; he had just kissed the tip of her cute little nose. But he just couldn't say what she wanted to hear. And yet, he couldn't let it just hang there between them. A dialogue over breakfast was just what they needed to clear the air.

He walked into the kitchen and stopped in the doorway to watch her butter toast. Dressed in a T-shirt tucked into jeans that hugged her hips and legs, she made even that mundane chore seem sexy. Knowing he would hate himself later, he walked up behind her and put his hands at her waist, then nuzzled her neck.

"Mmm," she said dreamily, tipping her head to the side to give him better access. "Good morning."

"How did you sleep?" he asked, hoping her rest had been better than his own.

"Like a rock." She turned into him and automatically wrapped her arms around his waist as she nestled into his chest.

He told himself that it was wrong to pull her against him. He also knew after last night that he could never go back to not touching her at all.

She lifted her lips to his for a sweet, almost chaste kiss that left him wanting to turn up the heat, to get out of the kitchen and back to the bedroom. But this wasn't the time or place.

Apparently she felt the same, because she patted his tie and stepped back. "How do you want your eggs this morning?"

"Scrambled." Like his mind.

"Okay." She turned back to the stove and cracked some eggs into a bowl, then beat them with a whisk.

His gaze dropped to her shapely derriere, then lower to her legs. He remembered the feel of them wrapped around his waist just a few hours earlier. The reality of her gesture, drawing him deeper inside her, was even more wonderfully erotic than the fantasies he'd had since first laying eyes on her. He grew hard at the thought, and shifted uncomfortably. This line of thinking wouldn't get him anywhere.

She divided the cooked eggs onto two plates, added bacon, fried potatoes and toast, then set them on the table. "Coffee?" she asked.

"I'll get it." He poured himself a mug, then sat

down at the table across from her. *Here goes nothing,* he thought. ''About last night—'' He stopped as a sweet, contented smile turned up the corners of her full mouth.

She looked like a woman completely fulfilled by her husband. That was good news—and bad. Good because she'd taken to the marriage bed like a duck to water. He couldn't help being glad that he'd satisfied her so completely that she wouldn't look to another man—especially a cowboy—for fulfillment. And he had never experienced with any woman the satisfaction he had with Mattie last night.

But bad because there was more to this than just the physical. Her emotional needs were much more complicated. And so important.

''What about last night?'' she asked. ''If you need to lodge a protest, the complaint department is now open.''

''I would be a fool to complain about a night like we had.'' Her saucy grin made him throb with need. ''But we have to talk about what you said.''

''What? When?'' She took a bite of toast as her smooth forehead creased with a frown.

She'd said it several more times. The words came so naturally to her that he wasn't surprised she didn't have a clue what he was talking about. Coming from a big, loving family, affection had been a constant in her life. It was something taken for granted. He envied her; he hadn't been so lucky. His father hadn't been around much, and his mother had needed *his* emotional support after the divorce. She'd been in no condition to nurture.

''When I asked how you felt after we made love.''

''Which time?'' she asked, grinning wickedly.

"The first time," he said, exasperated because it was difficult to stay focused with her. Damn, she was distracting. He had to agree with her mother about naked arguing. It was sure to end any disagreement. "And I was talking about physically. But you said—"

"I love you," she interrupted.

"Right." He rested his forearms on the table and met her gaze. "I know you want me to say it back."

She stared at him for several moments, then shook her head and frowned. "I don't think I want to talk about this now."

Dawson squarely met her gaze. "Waiting won't make the problem disappear, Mattie."

"I never said it would. I just don't think this is a good time."

"It's as good a time as any. I believe in honesty and communication." *Unlike my father,* he thought. If his old man had just been honest with his mother, their whole sordid mess would have been easier to deal with.

"Honesty and communication are good. At a mutually convenient time."

"I'll make this quick. You said you loved me."

She nodded. "And I meant it."

He wanted to ask her why. He had taken her virginity and spoiled her for another man. He'd used her badly and forced her into marriage because of it. She had forfeited her hopes and dreams because of his baser needs. He couldn't believe that what she felt for him was love.

"I care about you—a lot," he said. "But I can't say that I love you." He winced as the light in her eyes seemed to flicker.

She looked as if he'd just hit her, and he felt lower

than a snake's belly. Then she lifted her chin and met his gaze. He couldn't help admiring her guts. She was a hell of a woman.

"I never asked you to," she said.

"But you want to hear the words."

"Every woman wants that," she said. "But not if you don't mean it."

"I care about you more than I've cared for any woman, Mattie."

She shook her head. "Don't lie to me, Dawson."

"It's not a lie. That's not my style."

She nodded, satisfied. "Good. I'll hold you to that and believe you care. It's a start. Love has grown under weirder circumstances."

He ran a hand through his hair. "That's just it, Mattie. I don't know what love is. I'm uncomfortable with the word."

"Okay. You don't have to say it. Just don't expect me to *not* say it."

"Can't we leave love out of this? We have something better."

"Better?" She looked incredulous. "What could possibly be better than love?"

He saw the look in her eyes and knew he'd made a serious error. He'd forgotten that this was the same woman who'd fantasized about a marriage proposal complete with candlelight dinner and her intended on one knee when he popped the question. She was a hopeless romantic dressed in denim instead of lace. The funny part was, he wouldn't have her any other way. Did that mean he loved her? He didn't know.

"I'll tell you what's better than love. Respect," he said, nodding emphatically.

"Respect?" She looked even more incredulous. In

fact, she looked like she might be contemplating slugging him.

He nodded. "I have learned to regard you with admiration and affection."

"If you can't love me, Dawson, at least have the guts to just say so. Don't throw twenty-dollar words at me and think that makes everything a-okay."

"That's not—"

"Don't interrupt. If you can't really care about me, don't tippy-toe around the issue and cover it up. Say it straight out."

There was a *honk* from outside.

"What's that?" he asked.

"My ride," she said, pushing her practically untouched plate of food away. She stood.

"I'm taking you to the ranch."

"Since when?"

Since last night. But apparently he'd forgotten to mention it to her. "I'll go out and tell whichever of your cowboy chauffeurs is waiting that I'm driving you in later."

She shook her head. "I'd rather ride with the devil himself. You can take your respect and stick it—" She stopped and took a deep breath. Her voice was sad when she said, "I'm going to work now. I hope you and your respect have a wonderful day." She half turned, then rounded on him again. "And I hope that respect warms your bed tonight."

Then she turned on her heel and walked out. Dawson started to follow, but the phone rang. He looked at it, then at Mattie's retreating back. He wanted to go after her, but couldn't ignore the insistent ringing. It could be news about Clint Lockhart. Until the man was caught, he wouldn't breathe easier about Mattie's safety. As much as he hated the idea of her riding to work with one of the ranch hands, it was better than her going by herself.

As he picked up the phone, he heard the front door slam, and flinched as the windows rattled. "Hello?"

"When did you plan to tell me that I have a daughter-in-law?" asked the familiar female voice.

"Hello, Mother." Dawson sighed as he took the remote receiver and sat in Mattie's chair. "How are you?"

"Fine. Actually, that's not entirely accurate. I'm miffed that you didn't see fit to let me know that you were married."

"How did you find out?"

There was a chuckle on the other end of the line. "So you're only sorry that you got caught."

"Yes, and that I haven't had a chance to fill you in. How did you find out?" he asked again.

"Mallory told her mother, who told a mutual friend, who mentioned it thinking I already knew." She tsked. "I nearly choked. A heck of a way to find out your only son is married."

So he'd screwed up. What else was new?

"Sorry, Mother. I'm not going to bore you with excuses."

"Are you even going to tell me her name?"

"Matilda—Mattie Fortune. She's from the Australian branch of the family."

"Tell me everything. And start with the excuses. I have a feeling they're the juicy part."

He picked up Mattie's fork and pushed eggs around her plate. "It was a whirlwind affair, and we got caught up in a double wedding ceremony with Mattie's brother Brody. I knew you were traveling and wouldn't be able to get back in time. Reed and Mallory are on their way to live in Australia, and we all wanted to get married while they were still here.'' He looked at the door his wife had slammed only moments before. ''And life with Mattie is never dull.''

''What's wrong, Dawson?''

He could almost hear a frown in his mother's voice. ''Nothing.''

Everything. His answer was automatic as it always was with his mother. He'd taken on the role of her protector and old habits died hard. But he couldn't help wondering how women were able to read him so well. Especially his mother. He was always the one trying to cheer her up. Get her over the depression and resentment of being dumped for a younger woman. Somewhere in all that, the dynamics of their relationship had shifted. He'd always felt like the parent, and she the child. He didn't think she knew him at all.

''Don't give me that 'nothing' garbage, son. I know I haven't always been there for you when you needed me. I apologize for that. But I'm here now. And I can hear in your voice that you're upset about something. Tell me what's really going on. What's bothering you?''

He'd told Mallory. What harm could it do to let his mother in on the sordid details? ''I married Mattie because I seduced her.''

There was a noise on the other end of the phone that sounded an awful lot like a snort. His mother never snorted.

''That happens all the time,'' she said. ''And men don't feel obligated to marry the woman.'' There was a pause. ''Is she pregnant?''

He hoped not. ''No. But she was a virgin.''

Another snort. "Pregnancy and virginity aren't mutually exclusive, Dawson. Your father, the doctor, was supposed to have explained all this to you twenty years ago."

He laughed. "He did. I know all about the birds and bees."

"Good." There was another pause on the line, then she said, "You know, son, you're a lot like him."

"Now there's a recommendation," he said wryly.

"You have no reason to believe me after all the disparaging remarks you heard about your father over the years. But he was a good man. Just like you."

Now it was his turn to snort. "Yeah. Hold on while I dust off my wings and halo." He heard her laughter.

"He was also flawed, just like you." She sighed. "Dawson, I'm a selfish woman. I've struggled with it all my life. It cost me your father, and I withdrew from you. He and I ran out of time to rectify the mistake. I won't let the same thing happen with you."

"What are you saying, Mother?"

"Your father and I started having problems because I demanded more and more of his time. He was a gifted heart surgeon who had an obligation to use his talent for saving lives. Selfishly, childishly, I asked him for more time than he had to give me. We quarreled constantly, and eventually he turned to someone else for solace and companionship. Probably sex, too."

"What's your point? I'm sure you have one, Mother."

"You bet I do. He came to me once after he'd married again. He asked what I thought about a reconciliation."

"What happened?" He knew his shock at her revelation was evident in his voice.

"I turned him down." Her voice caught, and she was silent for several moments. But emotion crackled through the phone line. Finally she said, "It was the second stupidest thing I've ever done in my life."

"What was the first?"

"Pushing him away with my constant demands." She sighed. "Dawson, he came to *me*. He admitted that he'd had a midlife crisis and took all the blame. He said that I was the great love of his life. But my pride wouldn't let me forgive him."

"Again, I have to ask what your point is, Mother."

"I hear something in your voice when you talk about Mattie. You've never sounded that way before when telling me about the women in your life. I suspect she's the one."

"The one?"

"Don't be dense, dear. The great love of *your* life. My neediness robbed you of your childhood. I won't let the lessons of my behavior cheat you out of the happiness you deserve. Make it work with Mattie. Bare your soul. Get in touch with your feminine side."

"I don't have one." He chuckled. "You've been taking psychology courses again, haven't you?"

"Yes, but that's beside the point. If your father was right, and I think he was, we only get one good shot at love. He and I had it and were too stupid to hold on to it. Don't repeat our mistake. Don't be like me. Don't miss out on life because of stupid, stubborn, senseless pride. Do as I say, not as I did."

Dawson rubbed his thumb over the tines of Mattie's fork, which he still held. "She told me she loves me.

The first words out of her mouth when she woke up this morning.''

''I hope you responded in kind,'' his mother said.

''Actually, I told her we had something better than love. Respect.''

''Dawson Geoffrey Prescott. I can't believe I raised such a dunderhead.'' She sighed again. ''We reap what we sow. Unfortunately, I sowed some seeds that made you far too cautious. I assume all the blame for your being relationship-impaired. Not to mention spontaneity-challenged.''

''Is that the diagnostic term for it now?''

''Sarcasm is so unattractive, dear. But it's my fault that you've messed up so badly. Maybe I can help. Put Mattie on the phone.''

''She's not here. She trains horses at the Double Crown, and she left a little while ago.''

''Then go after her, Dawson. Tell her what's in your heart.''

''I don't know, Mother—''

''Do it, son,'' she said. There was a thread of steel in her voice that he'd never heard before. ''I let pride and hurt tarnish all the good times your father and I had. Pushing him away condemned me to a life of loneliness without the only man I will ever love. Don't make the same mistake, Dawson.''

''I'll talk to her.''

''Good,'' she said firmly. ''I'm looking forward to meeting Mattie.'' She stopped for a moment, and he could almost hear her thinking. ''One more thing, Dawson.''

''Yes?''

"I love you."

That startled him. She didn't say that often. Neither did he. He hesitated for a few moments before answering truthfully, "I love you, too, Mother."

Fifteen

It was midmorning when Mattie found Lily Fortune in the great room at the Double Crown. She'd been unable to make any progress with the problem horse she'd been given to train. Her concentration was non-existent. Thanks to Dawson. Respect, indeed! How dare he insult her intelligence. At least her gut instinct told her he had. But what did she know about men?

How she longed for her mother to talk to, but she couldn't upset her family with a long-distance phone call. The next best thing was her aunt.

"Can I talk to you for a minute, Aunt Lily?"

The older woman turned. "Of course." She stood in front of the great room fireplace with garland in her hand. A Christmas tree, already decorated, graced a corner of the room. "I could use a break. Would you like a cup of coffee or tea?"

"No, thanks." Mattie shook her head. The thought of coffee turned her stomach. Usually she had a cast-iron constitution. Since she'd never experienced love before, she figured the queasiness was the way her body reacted to man trouble.

"What can I do for you?" Lily asked.

"If you were my fairy godmother, you could turn my frog into a prince," she said, trying to joke. She sat down on the leather couch facing the fireplace.

Lily walked around the coffee table and took a seat beside her. "What's wrong, dear?"

Mattie met the older woman's sympathetic gaze. "Since I was a little girl, all I've ever wanted was to love and be loved. And have a baby."

"That's what most women want. You've taken the first steps to make that happen. You and Dawson found each other and fell in love."

"That's just it," she said, twisting her fingers together. "We found each other, sort of. But we didn't exactly fall in love," she added, remembering his words that morning. Her heart wrenched with sadness.

"I've seen the way you look at him, dear. If it's not love, then I don't know what is."

"It's not me. It's him. He has this whacked-out sense of honor, and it's messed everything up. He makes my body hum, then breaks my heart. He talks about the 'right' thing, but it all feels so wrong." She felt a wave of tears cresting, and covered her face with her hands.

The couch dipped as the other woman slid beside her and put an arm around her shoulders. "Tell me everything."

That was all she needed to hear. Mattie lowered her hands and looked at her aunt. She told her everything that had happened to make her so miserable.

"And why did you agree to the marriage?" Lily asked after listening intently. "Given your attire at the wedding, I have a feeling no one could force you, or Dawson either for that matter, to do anything you truly didn't want to do."

Mattie sighed. "At the time, I thought it was because Griff threatened to go to my folks with the story. Now I realize that I'm in love with Dawson."

"So what's the problem?"

"He doesn't love me back."

"Are you sure about that?" Lily reached out and tucked a strand of Mattie's hair behind her ear. "I've seen the way he looks at you, too. It's not the expression of a man who has no feelings for you."

"Oh, he's got feelings, all right. Something better than love," Mattie said bitterly. "R-E-S-P-E-C-T."

"Did he tell you that?" Lily asked, astounded.

Mattie nodded. "This morning. In bed. After the most wonderful night I've ever—" Her voice broke, and she bit her lip to hold back the sobs.

"Blockhead," Lily mumbled, tightening her arm around Mattie.

"Exactly." Mattie sniffed. "So, I've been thinking, and I've come up with a plan."

"What?"

"I'll stay with Dawson a decent length of time to spare my parents the embarrassment of knowing what really happened between us. Then we'll split up and tell everyone it just didn't work out."

"Mattie, sweetheart, don't rush into a decision like that. It's only been three weeks since the wedding. You need to give the relationship time to grow. Unless I miss my guess, Dawson Prescott is very much in love with you. All this respect nonsense is a smoke screen. He's afraid to say the words."

"But why?"

Lily shrugged. "I don't know all the history. But I think it has a lot to do with his parents' breakup."

"Silly Aunt Lily," Mattie said fondly as she shook her head. "Thanks for trying to spare my feelings. And don't take this the wrong way, but I think you're mistaken. Dawson isn't afraid of anything. If he loved me, he would say so.''

''Sweetie, you grew up with five brothers, but you don't know squat about men. No offense. The men in this family, including Dawson, could face down a grizzly, go nose to snout with an alligator, wrestle a mountain lion to the death for the ones they love. But saying that one small four-letter word scares the hell out of them.''

''Aunt Lily!'' Mattie exclaimed in mock outrage. She grinned, and the other woman smiled in response.

''Just give it some serious thought before you do anything you'll regret,'' Lily said.

''I will.'' Mattie leaned over and kissed her cheek. ''Thanks. You're a terrific stand-in mom.''

''You're welcome.'' Lily hugged her. ''Anytime. And just you leave everything to me.''

''Leave everything to me,'' Mattie mumbled.

''What?'' Dawson asked, glancing at her momentarily, then back to the winding road he drove.

''Nothing. Just talking to myself.'' *For practice,* she added silently. Because she planned never to talk to anyone ever again. Her last bare-her-soul, heart-to-heart chat with her aunt had resulted in Ryan and Lily's thinly veiled plan to save her marriage.

Because of that conversation, Mattie now found herself sitting in Dawson's BMW on the way to the Fortune family cabin near a lake. It belonged to a friend of Lily's. Because of the threat Clint Lockhart presented, Ryan was concerned about sending them to the family cabin. He was afraid the deranged man might know about it. If Mattie had known the words ''Leave everything to me'' meant that her aunt and uncle would give her and Dawson a surprise honeymoon, she might have thought twice about spilling her guts to the older woman.

Last evening, Dawson had come to the Double Crown because he'd said he was worried when she didn't come home on time. Hah! Worry about someone you merely *respected?*

But Ryan and Lily had sat the two of them down and said that since they'd married so quickly and hadn't planned a honeymoon, they were to take it now. Ryan gave Dawson an executive order to take some time off, and insisted Mattie have a vacation from her work on the ranch. They were not to show their faces for at least a week.

And now they were stuck with each other. Alone.

"I think we're there," Dawson said.

He pulled the car into a drive and stopped beside a single-story wooden cabin. Through a thicket of leafless trees, Mattie saw the blue water of the lake.

They got out of the car and unloaded the suitcases from the trunk. Dawson had the cabin key and let them inside where they explored the fully appointed kitchen, living room with stone fireplace on one wall, and four bedrooms. It wasn't fancy compared to the Double Crown, but it was cozy and comfortable.

And far too isolated, Mattie thought. Not a computer or calculator, or horse and saddle in sight. Nothing to distract them or take the heat off.

But heat wasn't their problem. That's what had landed them here in the first place.

She noticed that Dawson put all their luggage in the same bedroom. Was that a good sign? She couldn't afford to let herself hope.

When they'd unpacked clothes and a week's worth

of groceries, they stood on opposite sides of the center island in the kitchen and stared at each other for a few moments.

"Now what?" she asked.

"Talk," he answered. "A person would have to be deaf, dumb and blind to miss what Ryan and Lily are doing."

"Marriage counselors," she answered.

He nodded. "Along with my mother."

"Your mother?"

"Yeah. Contrary to the rumor about me being discovered under a cabbage leaf, I actually have a mother. She called yesterday morning. Right after you left," he added. "She found out about our wedding."

"Is she upset?"

He shook his head. "She pretended to be miffed, but I'd have to say she sincerely wished us every happiness."

"We might be able to be happy. If we get a divorce," she said grimly.

"What?" he looked genuinely shocked.

"Obviously this marriage was a mistake."

"Obvious to whom?" he asked.

"I don't mean to sound ungrateful." She took a deep breath to ward off the pain of the heart-breaking proposal she was about to make. Quite different from the one she'd always dreamed of having from a man. "I think we should wait a decent interval and then separate. We'll tell everyone that it just didn't work out. The rest of the details are easy. I don't want anything. I'm just as responsible for this situation as you are. And I sincerely appreciate what you tried to do. But it just seems wrong for both of us to be unhappy for the rest of our lives."

"This is because I told you I respect you. Because I didn't say I love you." His shocked expression gave way to something that closely resembled anger. "That was stupid. But you have to understand something, Mattie."

"What?" she asked.

"I didn't grow up like you with a normal, loving couple for role models. My father left my mother for a much younger woman when I was ten. It was devastating for her, especially because she felt the age factor left her no weapons to fight with. From then until I left for college, I had my work cut out for me trying to undo the damage my father had done to my mother's self-esteem."

"I'm sorry, Dawson. It must have been horrible for you both to go through that. But I don't see—"

He held up a hand. "I'm not finished yet. All these years I blamed my father for using her, then walking out when he found a younger woman. But my mother told me yesterday that she bears some responsibility, too. She resented the hours he devoted to his patients, his being on call, his long office hours. She demanded more time than he had to give her. She constantly threw in his face that there wasn't enough of him left over for his family."

"I'm so sorry you had to deal with all that."

"I don't want your pity," he said angrily. "I'm just trying to explain that I don't know a lot about relationships. All I learned is that it's not easy to make it work when the people involved are so different. They suffer. And not just the ones *in* the relationship. It's the people around them. Kids."

"What are you trying to say, Dawson?"

He ran a hand through his hair. "I guess I'm trying

to say that two mismatched people have the deck stacked against them.''

Mattie felt as if he'd just stabbed her through the heart. Cupid would be hard-pressed to find a man and woman more mismatched than the two of them. The miserable look in his eyes confirmed her suspicions. He agreed that they should separate. Until that moment, she hadn't realized how much she'd wanted him to talk her out of her divorce idea. Or how deeply she'd hoped voicing it would shake him up and make him realize that he *did* love her.

But he agreed with her. The pain of losing Dawson, of losing the man she loved, settled around her heart like a stone. It took her breath away. Before she made a fool of herself in front of him, she needed to be alone to compose herself.

She turned away from him and headed for the front door.

''Where are you going?'' he asked. His tone smacked of surprise or annoyance, or both.

She didn't have the energy to care. ''I need some air. Please don't follow me. I'd like to be by myself.''

She walked outside and slammed the door behind her. The December wind made her cheeks tingle. For a few seconds she focused on that, rather than the fact that her heart was breaking. She knew there would never be anyone for her but Dawson. Her mother was a one-man woman, and Mattie had no doubt it was the same for her. How could she go on without him?

She saw a trail through the woods and started walking. Her pace was brutal, probably because she was trying to leave her demons behind. But as tears started to trickle down her cheeks, she knew she would never be able to outrun the pain of living without Dawson.

She brushed the moisture from her cheeks, trying to clear her vision and focus on the path in front of her.

The sound of a twig snapping behind her made her stop. Had Dawson ignored her request? Was he following? Foolishly she hoped that was the case, and waited for him to catch up. As she stood in front of a tree, she struggled to catch her breath. Suddenly a wave of dizziness swept over her, followed by a disorienting light-headedness. Blackness closed in, eating up the light. Her body felt heavy, and she felt herself falling.

At the same time, from a great distance, she heard an explosion. Then nothing.

Pacing the cabin like a caged tiger, Dawson heard what sounded like a car backfiring. Not likely, since this area around the lake was way too isolated for other vehicles. A hunter? The noise he'd heard didn't sound like a rifle. Could it have been a pistol shot? *Clint Lockhart?* That threat had been on his mind ever since the day he'd married Mattie and—

Another loud explosion rang out.

"Mattie?" he whispered.

Fear was a vise squeezing his chest as he raced from the cabin. Ryan had charged him with Mattie's safety, and he'd let him down. More importantly, he'd screwed up what he'd vowed to do. He'd left the woman he loved unprotected. He stopped and frantically looked around, cursing himself for not going with her. Which way had she gone?

"Mattie?" he called as loudly as he could. The echo of his own voice was the only response.

He saw the path leading into the woods and hoped to God it was the right way. He ran as if the hounds of hell were after him. His footsteps, pounding in the dry leaves on the hard ground, echoed the prayer that played over and over in his head. *Let her be all right.*

Although it seemed a lifetime, only several minutes passed before he saw her—collapsed on the ground at the base of a tree. Not moving. *Oh, God, please don't take her from me.*

He skidded to a stop, then went down on one knee beside her still form. With the threat of more gunfire, he couldn't stay out in the open. He scooped her into his arms and hunched his body around hers, trying to protect her as best he could. He ran with her a short way to a shallow ravine lined with rocks. He ducked behind them and slid the short way down the embankment, cradling her against him. His heavy breathing was the only sound he heard as he waited for more shots.

A few seconds later, he heard the snapping of twigs and the crackle of dead leaves. Someone was running through the trees. As the noise grew more faint, he realized whoever it was—Clint Lockhart, no doubt—was moving away from them. Then he heard nothing but silence and the occasional calling of a bird.

"Mattie?" Still holding her, he brushed silky blond hair back from her face as he scanned her from head to toe. Other than a nasty scrape on her cheek and a bump on her temple, he saw no blood or other sign of trauma. No gunshot wound. Her chest rose and fell, telling him that she was breathing. He sighed with relief.

He ran his hand over her arms and legs in a cursory examination. "Mattie? Sweetheart? Please wake up."

He heard the desperation in his own voice, and asked any god who would listen to an insensitive moron like himself to bring her back to him. He loved her. Although he didn't deserve to have his prayer answered, he begged for her to be all right.

He pleaded for the chance to tell her he loved her.

"Betsy Keene, small and mean." Clint Lockhart smiled.

Betsy shivered, as much from that creepy smile as his nasty little rhyme that he seemed to find so funny. It was a fact that she was small; some folks called her mousy. But she wasn't mean. She'd had a hard, lonely time of it was all. Now it was her turn to have something or someone.

She'd thought her luck was changing when Clint stumbled into her life months earlier. Men as handsome as sin didn't just fall off the turnip truck. But he had done practically that. Only difference was, it was a prison vehicle and he'd been wounded in the escape. But that didn't matter since he'd been framed by the Fortunes. Once he got even with Ryan Fortune, she and Clint could finally be happy.

Only, she had to tell him she'd screwed up that revenge.

She put her hand in the pocket of her worn jeans to hide the shaking. It had been like that ever since she'd fired off several shots at Matilda Fortune in the woods. At Clint's insistence, she had followed the couple from their house to the cabin.

Betsy closed her eyes at the memory. She still couldn't believe what she'd done. Now she was even more afraid. She had to tell Clint she'd failed to do as he'd asked.

She lowered her gaze, but managed to lift her eyes just enough to study him without his knowing. He was just about the best-looking man she'd ever seen. His blue eyes and reddish-brown hair and six-feet-tall muscular body set her heart to fluttering something fierce. In her forty-odd years, no man had paid her any mind. She still couldn't hardly believe that a man like him could be interested in a nobody like her.

She was scared to death that he wouldn't give her the time of day when she told him she failed at the latest errand he'd sent her on. She'd been frightened to do it, but more afraid not to. Now she pictured her future without Clint in it, and didn't like what she saw. She had no one without him. Her folks were dead and her brother was on the run from the law. She hadn't seen or heard from him in years.

She'd tried her best to do whatever Clint told her to do. But when she'd pointed that gun, her hands had been shaking so. No way could she hit anything she aimed at. How in the world was she going to tell Clint and make him understand? More important, make him still love her?

"So, Sugar, don't keep me in suspense. Tell me what happened. Tell me how you got even with the Fortunes for me. I want to hear all of it, every last detail. Then I can leave this country a happy man. Just you and me, Sugar. You followed them, right? They didn't spot you, did they? Did she see you? Did she know what was coming? Was she afraid?"

She licked her dry lips. Suddenly her legs wouldn't hold her. She dropped into one of the gray vinyl dinette chairs. She felt as old and worn as the chair with the stuffing leaking out the back. As old and worn as the scratched metal cabinets in her tiny trailer. As ugly as the orange-and-gold sofa that Clint told her was the most godawful piece of furniture he'd ever seen.

"Clint, I—" she looked down at her fingers twisted together in her lap "—it's like this—"

He turned away, rubbing his hands together in glee. "It would have been better if Ryan could have seen her get it. Or if she'd died in a hospital with him at the bedside, with nothin' he could do to save her. That would've been the best. But he's got that ranch so tight with security, you couldn't have done it there."

"Clint you gotta listen—"

He whirled around, startling her. But the hardness in his blue eyes made her cold all over. "Spit it out, woman. You did take care of her like I asked? Right?"

She swallowed hard. "The gun you gave me—" Just a little white lie. What could it hurt? "It— It wasn't real accurate." The truth was, the Fortune woman had dropped before she'd fired. Then there wasn't a clear shot.

His handsome mouth twisted into an ugly grimace. "You didn't kill the Fortune bitch?"

"No. She was walking so fast. Sh-She was crying."

"Damn you, Betsy. If you went soft on me, so help me I'll make you regret the day you were born."

"I—I wouldn't do that, Clint. I love you."

"At least tell me you hit her. If she hurts, Ryan Fortune will hurt." The narrow-eyed look he leveled at her was cold, hard and ugly.

"You gotta understand, Clint. It wasn't easy. I— I'm not real good with guns."

"So she doesn't even have a scratch." Angrily, he brushed his arm across the kitchen table and sent newspapers, beer bottles and day-old dirty dishes flying.

Betsy jumped as they crashed to the floor, glass shattering. "I'm sorry, Clint. I can—"

"You can't do anything right, you cow. You're so stupid, you can't walk and chew gum at the same time. I don't know why I trusted you to do anything so important." His chest heaved from his outburst. He took a menacing step toward her. "How could I love a woman as dumb and ugly as you?"

"I'm sorry. Please don't be mad, Clint."

Fear clawed her insides. Not fear of Clint. Fear of being alone if he left her. The thought terrified. Maybe if she'd never met him... She had to think of something. She needed a plan that would put her back in his good graces. A way to get even with the Fortunes. The best way was through someone Ryan cared about. Someone he cared about who didn't live at the Double Crown. Betsy remembered the way Ryan had fawned over his godchild, Willa Simms. And she lived in College Station. And maybe there was a way no one had to die. Maybe just make the Fortunes worry. A kidnapping. She remembered a movie she'd seen where kidnappers demanded a whole pile of money. That just might work.

"I've got a better idea, Clint," she said. She licked her lips. "We can't get Matilda Fortune now because they'll be guarding her like Fort Knox."

"So?" There was a hint of curiosity in his expression.

"So, what if we kidnap that Willa Simms girl?"

"What the hell good will that do?" he asked, exasperated. He rested his hands on slim hips.

Betsy warmed to the idea when he continued to look at her. It was a good sign. "Think about it. We take her, and let Ryan stew for a spell. Then we send him a note and ask for a whole lot of money so's we'll give her back." She stood up and took a step forward, trying to think fast. To come up with details she knew would appeal to him.

Slowly, thoughtfully he nodded. "Betsy, you just might have something there. With Double Crown security so tight, I can't get to a Fortune. Next best thing is someone Ryan cares about. Not only can I get even with him, but he'll pay to get her back. And I'll have me some money. The ultimate revenge, let Ryan Fortune bankroll my new life when I hightail it outta here. It's perfect."

"The trick is to ask for enough. Then you can take me with you." She forced herself to meet his gaze, hoping she would see agreement.

Clint smiled the deadly smile that meant he approved. Whether it was the kidnap plan, or her suggestion to take her with him, Betsy wasn't sure.

He walked over to her and stroked her cheek with one finger, then lifted her chin with one knuckle of his fisted hand. He smiled down at her. "Sugar, I just might keep you around, after all."

Sixteen

"How many times do I have to tell you I'm fine?" Mattie shook her head in exasperation as she stared at a pacing Dawson. She sat in the middle of their big bed in San Antonio. He had fluffed the pillows behind her back more times than she could count. "The doctor at the ER said I'm fine. There's no need for you to hover over me like a mother hen."

Silently she prayed that he would ignore her token protest. She liked all the attention he'd showered on her. She was storing up the warm, fuzzy memories for the long lonely days and nights that stretched in front of her. Days and nights without Dawson.

He stopped pacing and met her gaze, the look in his eyes making her heart pound. *"Au contraire,"* he said. The side of the bed dipped as he sat beside her, his bent knee just an inch from her thigh. "There are several excellent reasons for me to hover. I left you once, and someone took a shot at you. If Clint Lockhart tries anything else, he'll have to go through me. He is not going to get near you again."

The expression on his face was intense, angry and pretty darn fierce, she thought, going all gooey inside.

She couldn't help smiling. "If he knows what's good for him, he should be afraid, very afraid. And if he comes anywhere near Kingston Estates—" she pointed at him ''—one look at that face will send him running for cover.''

''If he comes near you again, I'll take him apart.'' He never raised his voice, but threads of steel ran through it. She'd never heard that particular tone before.

She looked at him and tipped her head to the side as she committed his features to memory. The intense hazel eyes. Tense, square jaw. Muscular body. She decided what she would miss most was his wonderful smell. Her hero. Her husband. Hers for this moment only. How she wished she could stretch it into a lifetime.

''Still,'' she said hedging, ''we don't know for sure that he was the one who shot at me.''

Dawson slid her a wry look that shattered his worried expression just for an instant. ''Who else could it be?'' He held up his hand. ''And don't give me your half-baked hunter theory. The cops dug a pistol slug out of that tree trunk. No self-respecting hunter would use a pistol. Not in Texas.'' He reached over and covered her cold hand with his warm one. ''That bullet hit the tree right about where your head would have been. If you hadn't fainted—'' He stopped and took a shuddering breath. ''I don't even want to think about what would have happened. Which brings me to the other reason I feel the need to hover.''

Knowing what was coming, she rolled her eyes. All the way home in the car he had asked every few minutes if she felt all right. Did she feel dizzy? Was she woozy? Was she awake? Maybe she shouldn't go to sleep. What if she had a concussion?

''I never faint,'' she said, heading off the barrage of questions. ''In all the years I've worked with horses, I've had much worse injuries, and I have never passed out in my life."

"Then how do you explain it? One second you were standing there, the next you dropped like a stone."

That was the question of the day. Maybe her small drugstore purchase would give her the answer.

Dawson had insisted on bringing her home to San Antonio when the police finished questioning them. She had asked him to stop at a drugstore for something she desperately needed. She'd only managed to stop him from accompanying her when she claimed embarrassment at buying some feminine items in front of him. Besides, she'd told him, even if Clint had ambushed her, it was unlikely he was anywhere around. And certainly not inside that particular store. Even at that, Dawson had stood guard at the automatic doors, and didn't relax until she and he were barricaded inside the house. Before they'd even arrived, he'd been on the cell phone to Sheriff Wyatt Grayhawk and arranged for law enforcement around the home.

Home.

She sighed. How quickly she'd come to think of it that way, in spite of the fact that she knew very soon she would have to leave it. And Dawson. Tears burned at the backs of her eyes—a frequent occurrence of late. If it was hormones on account of—

She wouldn't go there. Not unless she had to. If she found out for sure that her fainting spell had happened for the reason she suspected, this marital situation could get a whole lot more complicated. Dawson's noble streak had gotten them into this situation in the first place. His mother-hen syndrome told her his heroic hat was still firmly in place. If he found out *this* news, he would never agree to a separation.

More than anything, she wanted to be his wife and grow old with him. She loved him, more than she'd thought possible. But she didn't want him to stay with her out of a misguided sense of duty. He'd been the one who told her everyone around an unhappy couple suffers—especially kids.

"Aren't you planning to go into the office today?" she asked, anxious for some privacy.

"Are you crazy?" He looked at her as if she were. "Now who needs to have their hearing checked? I just spent the last five minutes explaining why I feel the need to hover. I am not leaving you by yourself."

"But I'm fine—"

"I don't care," he interrupted. "I mean, of course I care. I'm glad you're fine. But I am not leaving this house, or you. Besides, Ryan gave me an executive order not to be at the office for a week. When I called him about what happened at the cabin, he reminded me of his order. You can't get rid of me, Mattie. I will not leave your side."

"Well, I'm going to have to leave yours," she said, sliding off the bed. As she did, their thighs brushed and she could almost see sparks, almost feel the flames of desire lick her from head to toe. More than anything, she wanted to be in his arms.

But she forced herself to keep going. *Practice,* she thought. She would need to remind herself every day without Dawson to just put one foot in front of the other.

She walked across the room and, without looking back at Dawson, shut the bathroom door between them.

Dawson had insisted Mattie rest all afternoon. Her color looked strange to him, her cheeks were white compared to the usual rose. He had taken the opportunity to make a few discreet phone calls. He'd been planning a surprise for Mattie. Partly to take her mind off the danger surrounding her, but mostly because he'd been given another chance and he wasn't about to blow it. He just needed to set the stage.

While Mattie slept, he'd set up a table in front of the fireplace. He'd used candles, crystal and china. Nothing but the best for his bride. That meant he needed help with food. He'd called a restaurant in town and ordered dinner, which had been delivered a few minutes earlier. Now all he needed was Mattie.

He knew she would always be all he needed. If his luck held, he would find the right combination of words to convince her of that.

As if on cue, she walked into the kitchen, sleepily rubbing her eyes. His heart started to pound at the sight of her—silky strands of blond hair tousled from sleep, sweatpants hugging her luscious curves, T-shirt pulled tight across her breasts. He ached with need for her.

She yawned. "Who's coming to dinner?" she asked, sniffing the delicious aromas while looking around at all the preparations.

"I hope you are."

Suddenly the drowsiness vanished, replaced by wariness. "You did all this for me?"

"I did. Now go sit down by the fire where it's warm. I'll bring dinner in."

"Okay," she said in a voice that told him she didn't trust everything not to disappear.

Dawson fixed two plates—lasagna, salad, garlic bread. He tucked a bottle of Merlot under his arm and took everything into the family room. Mattie sat there in front of a roaring fire, the flames' glow turning her hair to burnished gold. She had never looked more beautiful to him.

He set the plates down then opened the wine and poured them each a glass. He picked his up. "Let's drink to second chances," he said.

She hesitated a moment before picking up her glass. "Whatever you say," she answered.

When she didn't drink, Dawson was afraid his come-to-realize had come too late. Still, there were a few things he had to get off his chest.

Dawson put his glass down and covered her hand with his own. "Mattie, there's something I have to tell you." She stared at him and he knew she was listening intently. He took a deep breath. "You didn't let me finish what I was saying in the cabin."

"When?" she asked, her brow wrinkling.

"I told you my parents were mismatched, and in your usual impetuous, wonderful way you jumped to the wrong conclusion."

"Okay. Then tell me the right conclusion."

"My mother shared with me something that she discovered about her and my father. She said when you find the great love of your life, don't let go. Don't let pride or anything else tear you apart."

"But you said they were wrong for each other. That she demanded more time than he had to give."

He nodded and nervously twirled his wineglass. "She found out too late that she would have been happier with the small amount of time he could give than not having him at all. She told me not to make the same mistake."

Mattie's gaze narrowed on him. "What are you try-ing to say?"

He drew in a deep breath as he rubbed his jaw. "When I heard that gunshot and found you on the ground—" He shook his head. "I've never been so afraid in my life. I thought I'd lost you. My life flashed before my eyes—a life without you—and it was worse than anything I could imagine." He shook his head. "No, only one thing would have been worse—not tell-ing you how I feel."

She turned her hand palm up and linked her fingers with his. "Tell me now, Dawson. How do you feel?"

"I love you, Matilda Theodora Fortune Prescott." The words came out easily, after all.

Her eyes widened. "You picked a good time to call me that. I'm too stunned to retaliate."

"It's true. I fell in love with you the first time I set eyes on you, I just didn't know it. I love your spirit and your courage. Not a day will go by for the rest of our lives that you won't know how very glad I am that you're mine. I want to grow old with you." He laughed. "Older than I am now, anyway. I want to have children with you. As soon as possible. I'm not getting any younger."

Mattie stared at him. She blinked three times to make sure she wasn't dreaming. He had just said he loved her. Who knew that out of something so violent and frightening, a fantasy so wonderful and beautiful could come true?

"If I'd known it would take getting shot at to bring you around, I'd have done it sooner," she joked. "I have something—"

"That's not funny." He scowled.

"Lighten up, Dawson. Don't you see? I love you, too. You need to know—"

"Then why didn't you drink to second chances?" he asked, staring at her untouched wineglass. "If we're okay, it's customary to drink to the toast."

"That's what I'm trying to tell you." She squeezed his hand. "It's about all those children you want. I think we…got a jump start. It could be sooner than you thought."

He stared at her for a moment, then a slow, sexy, wonderful smile turned up the corners of his mouth. "Are you saying what I think you are?"

He actually looked happy. *Life just doesn't get any better than this,* she thought, grinning back. She nodded. "Why do you think I made you stop at the drugstore?"

"So the female stuff was a pregnancy test? You should have told me."

"I didn't want to say anything until I was sure. But I've been feeling sort of sick for the last few days. And when I fainted—" She stopped, realizing the magnitude of it all.

"The baby saved your life," he said, putting her thoughts into words. He was beside her in a heartbeat, down on one knee with his hand gently, protectively covering her abdomen. "This tiny miraculous result of our love actually saved your life—" His voice cracked. "I can't believe you were talking about a divorce."

"It was all that respect malarkey. I thought it was your way of saying you could never love me."

"You were wrong. I was just afraid to tell you I love you. Big difference."

She covered his hand with her own as together they

protected their child. "I can't wait to meet your mom. She's a very wise woman, and I think I'm going to like her very much."

"And she's going to love you. She'll be thrilled about becoming a grandmother." He reached into his pocket and pulled out a velvet jeweler's box.

Mattie's smile grew wider. It was a small box—the best kind. "Is that what I think it is?"

"You one-upped me with the news about the baby. But I'd planned to do this, and I learned the hard way that there's no time like the present." He opened the box, then lifted her left hand and slipped on a diamond engagement ring. "This ring was my grandmother's. It symbolizes to me that love has no beginning and no end. It's as strong and precious as the diamond at its center. For a methodical man, I've managed to do everything backward—mating, marriage, courtship. This proposal is a little backward and a bit late, but the sentiment is heartfelt and sincere. Will you be my wife?"

"Yes. I had just about given up on my fairy tale." She grinned down at him—the wavery him that she saw through tears of happiness. "I don't just mean the bent-knee proposal. All I've ever wanted is a loving relationship and children. You've given me both. Without a doubt, I am the happiest woman on earth. I love you with all my heart, husband."

"I love you more, wife."

"I plan to spend every day for the rest of my life making you happy. Here's a sample." Mattie leaned down and kissed him. She pulled back and smiled. "That first time in your arms was a night I'll never forget."

"Do you want to thank Griff, or should I?" he asked.

She laughed. "Thanks hardly seem adequate considering what he gave us. It was a very special night."

He stood and pulled her to her feet. "There are more where that came from."

"I'm counting on it."

Arms around each other, they walked down the hall to their bedroom. Mattie's heart was so full of happiness she felt it wouldn't hold any more. She was the luckiest woman in the world. One night of beauty had made all her dreams come true.

* * * * *

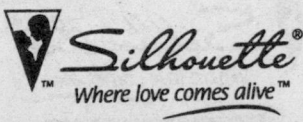

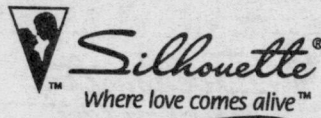

Forrester Square

LEGACIES · LIES · LOVE ·

The mystery and excitement continues in May 2004 with…

COME FLY WITH ME
by
JILL SHALVIS

Longing for a child of her own, single day-care owner Katherine Kinard decides to visit a sperm bank. But fate intervenes en route when she meets Alaskan pilot Nick Spencer. He quickly offers marriage and a ready-made family… but what about love?

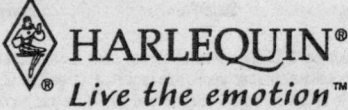

HARLEQUIN®
Live the emotion™

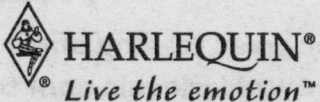
9/07

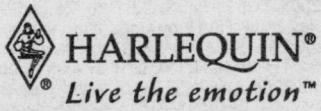

Coming in May 2004 to Silhouette Books

USA TODAY BESTSELLING AUTHOR

BEVERLY BARTON

CHECK MATE

When Jake Ingram is taken captive by the Coalition, a sexy undercover agent is sent to brainwash him. Though he finds her hard to resist, can he trust this mysterious beauty?

Five extraordinary siblings.
One dangerous past.
Unlimited potential.

**Look for more titles in this exhilarating new series,
available only from Silhouette Books.**